"I can't marry you ~~~ engagement over, ~~~ through the door.

Stunned, it took a moment or two for her words to sink in. The engagement was over? His plan had completely backfired. He lunged toward the door, but a big youthful waiter grabbed his arm.

"You haven't paid, sir," he said, voice deep to match his size and the strength of his grip.

Paul dug in his pockets to find his wallet, grabbed a wad of cash and pushed it at him, then sprinted for the door. "Brynne!" he yelled as he took two steps down at a time, and she backed out of her parking spot. "Brynne!" he called again as he ran toward the car that pushed on the gas and nearly fishtailed out of the driveway.

* * *

THE TAYLOR TRIPLETS:
Once lost, now found!

Dear Reader,

Have you ever wondered why some people are reluctant to tie the knot? Usually it's the guy putting on the brakes, but in *The Reluctant Fiancée* it's Brynne Taylor, the bride-to-be. She's a woman with a lot on her plate since becoming engaged. Just when her fiancé, Paul Capriati, decides to do something drastic to get his stalled-out wedding plans back on track, the unimaginable happens.

When I proposed the Taylor sisters to my editor, I had twins in mind...until there was room for one more. That set my brain on fire with ideas. So picture a certain bride-to-be having enough trouble dealing with her future husband, who is beginning to worry he'll never be a husband at all, and add to that hot mess not one, but two identical sisters. Sisters who suddenly show up wanting to get to the bottom of the mystery of why they'd been separated at birth. Then I ask, do you hear wedding bells in Brynne's future?

Hopefully you'll read *The Reluctant Fiancée* and see how it all works out.

Happy reading,

Lynne

LynneMarshall.com

The Reluctant Fiancée

———

LYNNE MARSHALL

HARLEQUIN
SPECIAL
EDITION

HARLEQUIN®
SPECIAL EDITION™

Recycling programs
for this product may
not exist in your area.

ISBN-13: 978-1-335-89456-4

The Reluctant Fiancée

Harlequin Enterprises ULC
22 Adelaide St. West, 40th Floor
Toronto, Ontario M5H 4E3, Canada
www.Harlequin.com

Printed in U.S.A.

Lynne Marshall used to worry she had a serious problem with daydreaming, and then she discovered she was supposed to write those stories down! A late bloomer, she came to fiction writing after her children were nearly grown. Now she battles the empty nest by writing romantic stories about life, love and happy endings. She's a proud mother and grandmother who loves babies, dogs, books, music and traveling.

Books by Lynne Marshall

Harlequin Special Edition

The Taylor Triplets

Cooking Up Romance
Date of a Lifetime

The Delaneys of Sandpiper Beach

Forever a Father
Soldier, Handyman, Family Man
Reunited with the Sheriff

Her Perfect Proposal
A Doctor for Keeps
The Medic's Homecoming
Courting His Favorite Nurse

Harlequin Medical Romance

Summer Brides

Wedding Date with the Army Doc

Visit the Author Profile page
at Harlequin.com for more titles.

To surrogate mothers who help others
fulfill their dream of having a family.

Chapter One

Brynne Taylor sat across from her fiancé, Paul Capriati, on a late-afternoon Saturday date at the Rusty Nail. The restaurant was located out of town, off the highway, nestled against the copper-colored hills accentuated by the amber hues of early September and the pine green of cedars. The golden-colored knotty pine–paneled walls were decorated with buffalo, mountain goat and assorted deer heads, and there wasn't a single cozy booth to relax in, yet Brynne and Paul continued to go back time and again. It wasn't the most romantic place in the world, or convenient, but it was where they could depend on a good steak and a decent grilled salmon meal.

This part of Utah wasn't a sophisticated hub,

its ancestors being rugged ironworkers who built log cabins and learned to survive tough winters. But being the entryway to the state's great national parks, the scenery was nothing short of gorgeous and the air pristine. And Cedars in the City, population thirty thousand, prided itself on being a festival city, Shakespeare being their number-one event. It began in June and continued through September at the local university, where Paul worked. A festival of plays and a championship rodeo helped round out the continual tourist appeal.

"How's the steak?" Brynne asked, sensing something more than food was on Paul's mind.

"As always. Good." Yet he put his fork down, and stared kindly at her with his large hazel-brown eyes.

"What?"

One side of his mouth lifted, creating a look about her passionate professor of history she'd come to adore over the past two years. "It's been six months."

Ah, but this topic, she did not adore. "Since my mother died," she finished his sentence. Mom was the only relative she'd ever known, having never been told about or met her maternal grandparents. A father had never been discussed beyond where she'd gotten her copper hair, even when Brynne had asked straight out. She likewise put down her fork, knowing the topic of conversation would soon change and would require her undivided attention. Because she also knew what he wanted.

Paul surprised her, reaching across the table for her hand, squeezing. "You look beautiful today."

He always liked when, instead of her usual single braid down the back, she wore her hair up in a twist, allowing him the pleasure of undoing it later, when they made love. Though today he'd have to wait until much later, due to a reading at the bookstore.

She smiled coyly. "Thank you. And…?" Knowing without a doubt what he'd bring up next.

"And I want to marry you. You know that."

"We *are* engaged." For a year and a half! She lifted her left hand to show the beautifully set diamond, the ring that waited for its mate.

"But not married." He let go of her hand. "Look, I know it's been hard for you, losing your mom. I understood why we needed to cancel the wedding. But glance outside. Fall is practically here, and who wants a winter wedding in Utah?"

Spring had been their first choice, and the plans had been put into action last January for mid-March, but then her mother contracted a virulent, fluke virus that wound up killing her within two weeks. Shocked and devastated, they'd canceled the wedding. She'd had to quit the job she loved at the hospital and dive into helping Rory, her mother's business partner and closest companion, run the bookstore. From as far back as she remembered she'd wanted to be a nurse. Never a businesswoman. But since Mom died, that obligation had to come first.

Brynne had been flailing on all levels since. Especially where Paul was concerned. Of course she loved him, but he had expectations about marriage and family that sometimes sent shivers through her. If she said *I do*, she'd be obligated to give him the family he'd always wanted. One big like his, not like the old saying she preferred, "and baby makes three." They'd supposedly worked out their differences before their originally scheduled wedding, but since her mother died, for the life of her, Brynne couldn't remember how or why she'd agreed to his wishes. Her foot pressed against the wood planked floor as though it was a car brake.

"We could wait for next spring?" She'd try the hopeful route, one that bought her more time. His long Roman nose twitched, a sure sign he didn't like her answer.

"I don't want to wait anymore."

"You can move in with me?" How many times would they have this conversation?

"We already discussed this. Sleeping over was one thing, but moving in wouldn't be at either your house or mine, but ours. A new place. A place we'd make our home. Together."

She shook her head, her stomach beginning a familiar pinch whenever this conversation got rehashed. "I don't have time to house hunt now. It's taking every single minute to figure out the bookstore business."

"Rory knows how things work, doesn't she?"

His expressive eyes revealed he didn't understand. Would he ever?

"You know how Mom was—a total control freak, and private as all get-out."

So private that sometimes it almost felt like her mother was running from something, and hiding, as though looking over her shoulder. She picked at her paper napkin with the Rusty Nail restaurant logo on it. "You'd think Rory would know the biz inside and out, but… Not to mention the fact she took Mom's death worse than me. You know how tight they were. She's been depressed and forgetful, and so, so sad, since. I think she's completely forgotten how to smile."

"But she'd worked there for, what twenty years?"

"It's not the same, and that leaves me grappling to keep things going. For Rory's sake, and all of Mom's hard work."

"You sure you're not just being nitpicky, like your mother was?"

"You think this is a case of fruit not falling far from the tree, huh?"

"You do have your control tendencies."

It irritated her when he was right, and she couldn't deny her being extra hard on Rory had something to do with wanting to run the bookstore by the book, like a nurse would, when Rory had a more laid-back style, as in completely unorganized. "You think so? Why?"

"Because you're your mother's daughter, and

you're meant to be a nurse, delivering babies, not running a bookstore."

"Yes, well, I'm on my sixth month of leave of absence now. I think they may fill my position."

"They'd take you back in a heartbeat." He sighed, clearly frustrated as he often was when talking about rescheduling their wedding. "And you are doing a fantastic job of keeping the only indie bookstore in the city open. Though I do wonder at what price." There was never any doubt that he believed in her, just not in waiting until she felt ready to walk down the aisle.

She'd been thrilled about their wedding plans, couldn't wait to tie the knot, but then Mom died, and she couldn't disconnect those sad thoughts from her wedding. *It's that her death is still too fresh in my mind. I'd be walking down that aisle thinking of her instead of you. And on our day, I only want you in my thoughts*, she'd told him the day they'd canceled without rescheduling their wedding. The day she'd officially begun her sabbatical from nursing—and marriage.

"I've taken on the bookstore in honor of my mother's memory." How many times did she have to say it before she'd believe this was what she was meant to do? Her appetite took a hike.

"I understand. She deserves it."

"The city needs it."

"True, but I also know how close you two were. I can only imagine how much loss you feel."

Then why, on so many levels right down to her gut, did she question if she knew her mother at all? There were so many unanswered questions about her life before Brynne had been born. Questions that would never get answered because she didn't have any relatives to ask. Though Mom and Rory were closer than close—a hunch Brynne had never had the nerve to verify—even Rory didn't know the answers. She focused back in on Paul, who was watching her in all earnestness. She could practically read his mind.

What about you? Don't you deserve your own life? With me? She waited for Paul to repeat his usual comeback whenever this stalled out marriage topic came up. He was a great guy, and understanding, but how could she explain this to him? Now that she was an orphan, she just wasn't ready. Not yet. The thought of starting a family without her mother's support and backup, seemed overwhelming. After a beat, surprised that he hadn't said his usual spiel, she pushed some steamed vegetables around her plate before peeking at him again.

At first Brynne was distracted when he tilted his head and a wave of his thick brown hair fell over his forehead. Then, without a thought, he brushed it back. He really did take her breath away. He deserved some kind of response. "And you're the most wonderful man I could ever hope for. I love you, Paul, but that bookstore is a mess." *It's not just my responsibility to the bookstore that's holding me back. It's also partly you...and me...and all those babies you want. How could they discuss such a topic in a public restaurant?*

Had she said bookstore out loud? Oops, wrong strategy with a man who lived to solve problems. One who'd thought they'd already worked out the first part about babies before they'd scheduled their wedding.

"You employ young, bright minds from the university," he continued, "who could probably step up and help you. You're underutilizing them. Why not make Nate, the business major, a manager, put his passion for success to work in your favor?"

"It all sounds lovely, but who has time to train anyone?"

"Which is why I'm suggesting we elope."

What? "That came out of nowhere."

His hand was back squeezing hers. "We could go to Vegas, get hitched and be back in time for my Monday classes and your normal business hours."

"And face the wrath of your family?" *His big fat Italian family who always found a reason to throw a party?* She'd never hear the end of it if they eloped, and who wanted to get off on such a wrong foot with future in-laws?

"Under the circumstances, they'd understand."

"No." She shook her head. "They wouldn't." She stared at him, seeing disappointment in the slant of his mouth. Would he give up on her if she kept coming up with excuses to postpone their wedding?

"Just give me a little more time, please. I can't leave town right now—there's too much going on with the store." *I'm still grieving.* This time she squeezed *his* hand. "A winter wedding could be an adventure." If she gave him a crumb, would he leave this topic for now?

"What would change between now and then?" He sat back in his chair, their hands only connected by fingertips now. "What's the real reason you don't want to marry me?"

Her neck stiffened, and her brows crashed down. "Do I need another reason than mourning my mother and trying to keep her lifelong business afloat?"

"Neither of which have to do with me."

He knew her too well. Knew her private history, except for one part—who her father was. As soon as she found out, she'd fill him in; it was an unspoken promise. He knew how Jessica Taylor had raised Brynne alone and taught her never to be dependent on anyone. Especially men. That was a topic Mom had never wanted to discuss on a personal level, leaving much to Brynne's imagination. Was it because of experience or preference? The question she'd never have the chance to ask.

Truth was, the thought of marrying Paul, a man who wasn't afraid of emotions and who wanted a lot of kids, scared the daylights out of her. They'd floated the idea of children before their planned wedding, and she'd been willing to make a go of it.

One baby at a time. Then her mother died, and the thought of handling a family without her mother's backup along with Paul's seemed overwhelming.

Paul knew she had every intention of continuing to work at the hospital, how could she do it all? Not to mention how he was an extrovert and loved his big gregarious family, and she was a wallflower by nature and had always been used to a quiet life with just her mother and her. As an introvert, the thought of constantly having to be around people, his people, drained her to near empty. Since "her people" only consisted of her mother and Rory, she was ill-prepared to go big in every way. These issues had become clearer since her mother died. It seemed, since then, she'd lost all of her confidence.

Could she handle a busy life with Paul?

"I love you, Paul, I swear I do. You're the most caring person I've ever met, and you're sexy and attentive. I couldn't ask for more." Yet there was something else she couldn't put her finger on. Brynne twisted the engagement ring around and around her finger. The fact she'd had zero experience with marriage of any kind was a major reason. Her mother had stayed single. She didn't have a clue how marriages worked. Fear of the unknown, like a sick metastasis over *not* having what it took to make a relationship last, invaded Brynne's mind. Failing at marriage would be too much to deal with. The fact she'd only had a handful of boyfriends before

Paul, all short term and forgettable, kind of proved her lack of expertise.

But he was different. So different. What if she hadn't been floated to the emergency department two years ago on the night he'd come in with food poisoning? Talk about an unglamorous way to meet. Still, even sick as a dog he was such a gentleman and he'd captured her interest. "I just don't think it would be wise to jump into marriage right now." Her being in deep mourning, frazzled over the bookstore, and missing her old job, could start them off on the wrong foot, and would they ever recover?

Paul shook his head, not buying Brynne's excuse for a second, and he worried what it might mean. With each passing month since their postponed wedding, he'd lost a little more of her. Was she finally going to dump him? If so, wasn't it time to intercede? "We've been dating for nearly two years—it's not like we don't know each other." They also had a very satisfying intimate relationship, one he'd never dreamed he'd find with a woman. Sex with his beautiful copper-haired Brynne was beyond compare.

"We've always had busy schedules," she continued, "what with your classes and my labor and delivery shifts."

He loved how she'd prided herself on being an RN at Cedars in the City Hospital, being willing to take any shift thrown her way. She'd always said it was to help save for their wedding. Now he wondered, what wedding? "Yet it's been even harder since you took over the bookstore."

Frustration was obvious in her expression, her eyes evading his. Maybe he was pushing her too hard, but he was desperate to get married, to start their lives together. He'd waited long enough.

"I've already explained I'm on a steep learning curve, just trying not to fall off."

In his mind, if she loved him the way he loved her, she'd quit making excuses about one day spending their lives together, and just do it. Now. There was only one way to find out if she felt the way she'd just promised. Well, maybe he wasn't being the most understanding fiancé in the world, but Brynne could mourn her mother and be married and have his arms to comfort her every night of the week. Didn't she understand that? He wanted to marry the woman. "Then if you won't elope, here's another idea. My final idea." He wasn't usually the dramatic type, but some things, like stalling out on their marriage, called for extreme action. He desperately loved her, never wanted to lose her and honestly didn't know what else to do.

"It doesn't have to be big—hell, we can go to the judge's chambers and sign a license. But if you can't even agree to that, I don't know what else to say except…we're done." Had he just issued an ultimatum? It'd slipped out of his throat like razors before the idea and its repercussions had fully formed, and now it was too late to take it back. His heart raced and his palms got damp, yet now that he'd said those despicable words—*we're done*—he was determined to stand by them, swearing they needed to be said to jolt her out of the resistance. For her to see what she could lose.

As expected, or at least hoped for, shock overtook her face. His heart sank a little deeper inside. Her crystal-blue eyes first widened with alarm then narrowed with disbelief. A bolt of fear arrowed straight to his chest. *What if she leaves me?* Now his upper lip went moist, and panic set it. He'd done a terrible thing, and if the shoe had been on the other foot, he'd have been pissed. Really pissed. But wasn't that what she needed, an emotional shakeup to snap her out of it? All he could do was hope he hadn't completely blown it, or prepare to grovel if he had.

"You're dropping one hell of a bombshell," she muttered, clearly baffled and defeated, when he'd expected her anger.

He needed to walk it back. "I'm sorry, but I'm standing by it." Yet for some crazy reason, he'd doubled down instead! Damn, he was desperate.

He felt like a total tool, leaning so hard on her about their engagement and marriage at such a difficult time in her life, but it was too late. He'd said the words, and she'd recoiled instead of fighting back. A bad sign. Yet history always proved winners were those who stayed on course. If they were truly in a battle for their love, he'd fight and fight hard to win. To win her.

She glanced at her watch, a disturbing stillness settling over her. What would he do if he lost her?

Grovel. Definitely. Until she took him back.

"And you know perfectly well we met early for dinner because I have to get back to the bookstore to set up for the monthly author readings." She'd clammed up avoiding the subject and ignoring their huge problem, and it was his fault for pushing too hard.

"Which means?" he asked tenderly, hoping to keep the line of communication open, even after being the one who slammed the door.

"I have to go."

Couldn't she see there were other ways around this martyr role? "Another perfectly easy job to delegate to one of your university student employees." Evidently tonight, while thinking one way, with love filling his heart, everything that left his mouth showed no mercy. A true sign of a mixed-up and desperate man.

"Not so." She bristled, finally showing some emotion. "There's a lot more to do than just set up chairs." She was angry, and he was in her line of fire. At last. Maybe she'd finally take notice how frustrated and hopeless he'd become with their situation.

"I was just making a suggestion." His Italian family was big on theatrics and loud debates, but he'd learned to tone things back with the quiet and tenderhearted Brynne. Guilt ran roughshod over his hard-core sneak attack. He'd let his feelings and fears take over and had caused pain to the person he loved more than anything or anyone in his life. His gut coiled tight as he frantically searched for a way to make things immediately better.

She inhaled and forced a quick recovery. "I wish we had more time to talk, but I've got to leave." She stood while he wrestled for a way to smooth things over. "Thank you for dinner." Half of which she'd left on her plate, having not taken a bite since he'd brought up the mother of all touchy subjects: their wedding.

He tipped his head, holding his breath.

She stepped closer to him before he had a chance to get up, bent and gave his cheek a chaste kiss. "'Bye," she whispered above his ear, when he'd expected a *screw you*. Though that wasn't her way—he knew as much, even though he deserved it.

They hadn't accomplished anything today.

His hand shot to her wrist and grasped it, holding her there while he stood. "I'm sorry I've upset you," he said, cupping her face. "I love you so much—don't ever forget that." Then he kissed her with all the passion stirred up by their situation. A desperate and demanding kiss took over, and she seemed instantly all in. Paul didn't give a damn about their public display of far more than affection. If people wanted a show, he'd give them one. His pulse shot up when her arms clamped around his middle as she leaned into him and deepened the kiss. Maybe he hadn't lost her today.

Too soon, she pulled away, her cheeks pink and nostrils flaring with each breath. He'd made her breathless. Good. "I've got to go."

He tenderly tucked a curl he'd loosened while they'd kissed behind her ear. Surely she could see the love in his eyes, see how desperate he was to marry her. To prove he wanted to be with her for the rest of his life.

"We're not done with this conversation." He spoke quietly before releasing her and walking her to the exit, evidently more than willing to be the guy who, when his back was against the wall, knew how to fight dirty. Even as he worried and every cell in his body tensed that he'd gone about this ultimatum business completely wrong.

"Oh, I think we are." She turned just before stepping outside. "You've left me no choice."

Fantastic, his ultimatum had worked!

"I can't marry you now. So consider the engagement over," she said, then rushed through the door.

Stunned, it took a moment or two for her words to sink in. The engagement was over? His plan had completely backfired. He lunged toward the door, but a big, youthful waiter grabbed his arm.

"You haven't paid, sir," he said, voice deep to match his size and the strength of his grip.

Paul dug in his pockets to find his wallet,

grabbed a wad of cash and pushed it at him, then sprinted for the door. "Brynne!" he yelled as he took two steps down at a time, and she backed out of her parking spot. "Brynne!" he called again as he ran toward the car that pushed on the gas and nearly fishtailed out of the driveway.

Lacy Taylor Winters, now Gardner, had never been to Utah before. Though nearly eight months pregnant, she'd insisted on accompanying Zack on the road trip to St. George to meet her in-laws on his dad's seventieth birthday. Now, a week after the celebration, and having loved every minute of meeting his family, they'd taken a detour to Cedars in the City. It was the day before they were set to leave for home, and Lacy had a chance for an afternoon by herself. Finally! Too bad she'd had to deal with those pesky Braxton-Hicks contractions all morning.

Zack and Emma were taking a father-daughter hike, and once Lacy dropped them off at the trailhead, she took the opportunity to explore the historic downtown area. Almost immediately after parking, she saw a sign on the front of a beige brick building—Taylor's Bookstore. With Taylor being the middle name she and her twin shared, how could she not go in?

Deciding to work her way around to it, she first stopped into a touristy trinket shop to find something fun for her eleven-year-old stepdaughter,

Emma. After making a purchase, she stepped outside to the golden late-afternoon sun, enjoying the huge surrounding hills and mountains covered in cedars and the freshest air she'd ever inhaled. Her enthusiasm must've woken the baby, who actively shifted positions, which set off another Braxton-Hicks contraction. Correction. Another in a series of Braxton-Hicks contractions. Par for the course these days. Since having them all morning, she really needed to notice if they were regular.

After a moment of standing still, holding her ever-growing baby belly, waiting for things to settle down, she continued window-shopping on Main Street. She had a whole month in her favor—why time these expected contractions when all they were good for was a preview of what would come? Next month. But when a second, stronger Braxton-Hicks kicked in, she opted to walk across the street to the park and sit for a while. Wasn't that what she'd learned about those annoying dress-rehearsal type contractions? *If you're being active and they happen, take it easy. If you're resting and they happen, get up and move around. And always make sure you're not dehydrated, which is the number one cause for setting them off.* At over five thousand feet elevation, walking in the sun, that was likely to happen.

After drinking a bottle of water and feeling refreshed, with the contractions calming down, she headed back down Main Street, her eyes still on the prize of that book shop.

Joe Aguirre, her twin sister Eva's husband, had helped them track down a woman named Jessica Taylor to this part of the country. She was a person of interest in their search for their surrogate mother. Granted, Taylor was a common name, but wasn't this bookstore a coincidence? Or maybe a sign. Of course, that wasn't the reason for this trip. Zack's parents and family were. The search for a long-lost birth mother was just an interesting aside, and they happened to be in the same county, so why not?

Ouch! Those dang contractions were becoming a nuisance, and now that she was far from the park, with the baby pressing down on her bladder, she needed a bathroom. All bookstores had them, right? Rushing—as fast as a pregnant woman in the middle of the third trimester could—toward Taylor's Bookstore, her only goal was to make it in time to use the bathroom without leaking.

She checked her watch as she strode straight toward the glass door. Hmm, it had only been two minutes since the last one. The old brick building was two stories, and she prayed the bathroom would be on the first floor. No way could she take the stairs or wait for an elevator right now. She needed a bathroom!

Pushing through the doors, she spied an older woman behind the counter on the right who seemed to be reading. The woman had bobbed nearly black hair that had a wide silver swath across the front and wore red Harry Potter–style glasses on the edge of her pointy nose. A long line of shoulder-high book and magazine shelves divided the entrance, where Lacy was, from the purchasing aisle, where the woman sat.

"Where's the bathroom?" Lacy asked, trying not to sound urgent.

The store clerk glanced up then quickly back at her reading material. Lacy was pretty sure it was a magazine. "Where it always is, darlin'" came the odd reply.

How rude. Didn't she know this was an emergency? Her glare darted around the store, there, straight back on the left. Lacy didn't have a moment to spare to call out the bookstore clerk. She'd deal with it on her way out when she made her purchases, which would be inevitable. After all, it was a bookstore.

Dashing the last few feet, praying the bathroom was more than a one-stall deal, or if it was, that it was at least vacant, she lunged, stretching her hand out to the doorknob, then twisted and flung open the door.

She didn't have to wait. Thank heavens!

Brynne was so angry, she'd had a stomachache the entire drive to the bookstore. An ultimatum? From Paul? She never would've believed it. Yet he'd said it and didn't back down, even though he first looked as shocked as she felt hearing the words. Soon, though, his eyes had hardened, and he looked so determined—desperate, even—that she'd been stunned. He'd thrown her off, knowing she had to leave, then threw another curve when he'd kissed her like he might never see her again.

That's when her mind snapped. How dare he do this to her while she was still in mourning?

Had she really broken the engagement? Her anger at Paul's despicable dare renewed with vengeance— you bet she had! And as soon as she had the chance, she'd take off the ring.

She'd left the restaurant in a red-hot haze, and with each mile closer to the bookstore, the anger turned to fury. Who did he think he was? Where was his compassion? He'd been so wonderfully un- derstanding all these months, then suddenly today he'd turned on her. An ultimatum? He could stick it.

The thought of adding a wedding to her plate of responsibilities nearly sent her driving off the road. Couldn't he understand life was complicated now, and when things settled down, then she'd recon- sider marrying him? But right now, the last thing she needed was his pressuring her to tie the knot. Who was this man, demanding a marriage one mo- ment and kissing her senseless the next?

Frustration boiling over, she let go a scream as she careened down the hills.

Finally arriving in town, still unnerved and jit- tery, she absentmindedly parked in front of the store instead of in the reserved stall in the back. That spot being the prized perk that came with the apartment above the bookstore. When she realized what she'd done, unwilling to correct her error as though it was one offense too many to deal with for the day, she stubbornly put some money in the meter and strode inside. One more thing to deal with later—move the dang car before she got a parking ticket.

Had she really broken up with Paul? She shook her head, let it sink in. Apparently, yes, she had. But where was the relief? From where she stood, every single thing felt worse.

From behind the counter, Rory looked over her red readers, did a double take and made a weird expression, which contorted her large agape mouth.

"What?" Brynne couldn't help sounding curt, but seriously, too much was going on. She didn't need to be looked at as if she'd grown two heads when she had a fiancé giving her an ultimatum and she still needed to arrange everything for the book readings later, due to Rory's bad back. At least Nate was coming in to help.

Lessons learned from being a nurse—her usual reaction to stress was to focus on one thing at a time, and right now it was the bookstore. Paul was left compartmentalized in the restaurant, with a shocked expression. Let him stew in his little ultimatum scheme. Now she was on the job and needed to focus. These book events drove more people to the store and kept them coming back, which meant more book sales. Bringing in the local students broke the pattern—instead of always making the university bookstore their go-to for reading material, they could come here. The key was to offer them something different, like author readings. Especially by authors of YA, Fantasy, and the occasional romance book. The effort would be worth it.

"Aren't you in the bathroom?" Rory said with an incredulous tone, still looking as though Brynne had arrived from outer space instead of the front door.

"What?" Brynne knew Rory was still lost without Mom, but had she gone off her rocker?

"Except your hair was down," Rory uttered, obviously confused and barely audible.

"Have you had a stroke?" Brynne had had it with the day. Things were simply too weird to deal with.

Rory came around the counter to look closer at Brynne just when they heard a loud moan in the bathroom that quickly escalated into a cry. "No!"

"What's going on in there?" Concerned, Brynne hiked her thumb toward the bathroom.

"You came in asking for the bathroom," Rory said, clearly not herself.

"I did not."

"I must be seeing things," Rory mumbled.

Brynne bolted toward the bathroom door and knocked hard, Rory right behind her. "Are you okay?"

"No," the quivery voice said. "I think my water just broke."

What else would happen today? Brynne forced herself into nurse mode, letting every other crazy little thing go. "I'm a labor and delivery nurse." *Or used to be.* "Open the door so I can have a look, okay?"

A second or two of silence passed, then the lock clicked, the handle turned and the door slowly opened. Concerned about a pregnant woman just having her water break, Brynne's first glance was to the floor and the pool of fluid for verification. It wasn't bloody. *Good.*

"Holy doppelgänger," Rory exclaimed from behind her.

Chapter Two

Stunned by the woman in front of her, Brynne gasped at coming face-to-face with her mirror image. Who was in labor! "Who are you?" she managed to ask, though her mind was doing loop-de-loops.

"Oh my gosh, you look just like Eva," the red-head said while grimacing and grabbing her bulging abdomen.

"Who's Eva?"

"My twin."

"But who are you?"

"Lacy Gardner, and I think I'm in labor. But it's too soon. I can't deal with a third twin right now."

"A third twin?" Could the day go any more haywire?

"I think we have a long story to share, but *ouch!*" Lacy ground out the words while clutching her protruding abdomen as she squinted her blue eyes tight. "Not now. *Ahhh!*"

"How early are you?"

"Four weeks."

Clicking back into action, thinking like a nurse, Brynne was able to drop the thousand questions in her head to help a woman in need. "Rory, hon, call 911. Hold on, Lacy. Breathe through the contraction—go *hee-hee-hee* now, and *hoo* when it lets up. I'm going to get a mat for you to lie on so I can check and see how far into labor you really are." For no logical reason, Brynne grabbed the stranger and hugged her tight, which seemed like hugging herself. "I'm here for you, and you're going to be okay. Let me close the store and lock the door first," she said, focusing on one task at a time while flipping the business sign to Closed just as a couple of customers approached. "Sorry! Emergency." Then she latched the door. Lacy continued to hee-hee. Then Brynne rushed to the display of yoga books with mats next to the counter, grabbed one and ripped it open while Rory made the emergency call.

"What should I tell them?"

"Woman in labor inside the store. Tell them it's preterm PROM." Brynne lunged and slid across the linoleum to where she'd left Lacy clutching the door handle, heeing and hooing near the bathroom.

"Something about a prom?" Rory repeated on the phone.

"Premature rupture of membranes!" Brynne called out. She unrolled and placed the mat on the floor where the carpet was, went back to the rest-room, and helped Lacy lie down as Rory gave their location information.

"Let's have a look." No way could she deal with the fact that the woman in labor was her double, not now, but there was one thing she could handle—she knew how to be an L&D nurse after eight years of experience. And she missed the excitement of it, though this, if it was a message from above, was going a bit overboard. She helped Lacy bend her knees then lifted her dress and quickly sucked in air at what she saw. "Tell them—" Brynne focused back on Lacy "—how long were you having con-tractions?"

"I was having Braxton-Hicks all morning, and then they got worse this afternoon." Obviously be-tween contractions, Lacy was able to explain a lot, hand gestures and all.

Brynne turned to Rory. "Tell them the mother is approximately eight centimeters! Then get some fresh towels from my apartment!"

"That was labor?"

"Looks like you've been in labor for a few hours. Do you have a high pain tolerance or something?"

"Felt cruddy all day but—" she moaned "—eee,

I'm feeling it now!" Lacy let go of a groan, which turned into a guttural growl.

The woman was clearly in transition, the final phase of the first stage of labor. "Don't push, not yet!"

Brynne stood and wept behind the viewing room window where a baby boy she'd delivered in her bookstore rested in the newborn nursery. She tried to make sense of the last four hours but couldn't come close. Out of the blue, a woman from another state who could be her double came to her bookstore and began labor. She'd learned the out-of-state part from Lacy's husband as they waited for her hospital intake. When Lacy mentioned in a by-the-way manner—during labor, of all things—"you look like Eva, my twin," Brynne had been too distracted to take it in. You mean there's another one? The whole encounter reeked of fate, which Brynne made a habit not to believe in. But, seriously? Since that moment, the hair on her arms had raised at least a half dozen times. Unable to stop it, she shivered while viewing the tiny little guy, her fingers mindlessly smoothing down her arms.

Everything was a blur after she'd seen the baby's head pushing its way out. On automatic pilot, she'd done everything she'd been trained to do as a labor and delivery nurse. Except without proper equipment and lighting and having to deliver a baby on the floor of a bookstore while using her personal towels to swaddle the newborn. A crazy thought struck her—she was glad she used a good fabric softener. The baby had been tiny and completely lost in the folds of the soft towel, but she needed to keep him warm. She'd held the hand of a woman she'd never met before, sobbing while Lacy held her baby for the first time on her bookstore floor. A baby boy with copper-red hair, like her own. A lot of it.

Emergency services had taken over from there, but, half-crazed from the adrenaline high of delivering a baby herself and the nonstop questions about who Lacy Gardner was and why she had been directed to the bookstore on this specific day, Brynne had pushed through the door, following the paramedic and EMT. She'd hopped into her car, suddenly grateful she'd goofed up and parked in the wrong place, then lined up behind the ambulance at the first intersection stoplight for the short drive to the hospital.

Brynne had called a man named Zack, Lacy's husband, as instructed by Lacy as she got rolled into the ambulance. She'd told him to meet his wife at the hospital. When he explained Lacy had the car, Brynne changed her bloody top and drove to the trailhead he'd described and picked him and his daughter, Emma, up. If Lacy was right, they were relatives, and she'd just delivered his baby, and, well, she already felt like a part of something. A family? The thought nearly made her lose control of the car.

Their confounded expressions at the sight of Brynne repeated the craziest part of the whole experience. Even more than a flash delivery in a bookstore. Could someone look exactly like someone else without being related? The statements and questions began while she drove the father and daughter to the hospital.

"You look just like my stepmom," the very talkative Emma kept saying in awe.

Zack stared at Brynne and shook his head in disbelief. "This can't be true."

"What?" Brynne begged to know what everyone else seemed to, still mostly in the dark and grasping for answers.

"Long story, and Lacy and Eva need to tell it to you, not me" was as much as she could get out of him.

She sighed. "You're freaking me out, but okay. So let's celebrate your new son!"

Now, two hours later, she stood between Emma and Zack, looking through the baby window, chill bumps flowing, while blubbering over the new life who'd weighed in at nearly five and a half pounds and four weeks premature. Emma snuggled close to her, which was strange, and Zack stood with arms folded, proudly grinning at his son.

"His name is Christopher," Zack said. "After my father."

"That's a wonderful name."

"We were supposed to leave for home tomorrow," he said with a solidly handsome grin. The man had some great dark blond hair, too. "Looks like we'll be sticking around some."

"For a preemie, your boy seems healthy and strong, but the pediatricians will follow up with everything. This is a good hospital." She glanced through the window at the NICU nurse, Eleanor, who raised a hand in greeting when she noticed Brynne. She hadn't been back in the hospital since her mother died, and it was hard. Though seeing old work friends was kind of nice.

"We can't thank you enough. This is definitely one for the books," Zack said. When they'd first arrived, the doctor and nurses needed to immediately check out Lacy and the baby, who'd had a short time to bond in the ambulance on his mother's chest. Brynne watched Emma after they'd arrived at the hospital so Zack could be with Lacy and the baby for a few minutes alone. Then, while the nurse helped Lacy freshen up in preparation for her first attempt to nurse, Zack had met Brynne and Emma at the newborn observation window, where they'd watched the nurse clean up his son before sending him back to momma.

His cell whistled. "'Where are you?'" he read the text aloud. "We better go" was all he said, Emma and Brynne knowing exactly what Lacy's message meant. It was time for Emma to officially meet her brother.

Brynne wanted with all her heart to tag along, but she knew well this was a time for the new family to bond. Brynne was still a stranger.

Just before parting ways at the elevator, Zack turned. "Uh, how can we reach you?"

"What's your number?" Brynne said, then texted him with her personal info before saying goodbye and taking the stairs.

Walking in a dream through the lobby, she heard her name.

"Hey, Brynne!"

It was one of her coworkers waiting for the elevator. "Samantha, hi!"

"When are you coming back?" She put her foot in the elevator to keep the door open.

"No plans yet." Just being here again caused nostalgic pangs. Wasn't this where she belonged?

"Thought you should know they're training someone now."

There was no way she could go back to the grind of being an L&D nurse and run the bookstore—oh, and get married or else! Yeah, that job was over. "Thanks for the heads-up." Disappointment dripped over her.

"We miss you," said the short, plump mom and ace nurse in pink-patterned scrubs.

"I miss you guys, too." It wasn't an obligatory response; it was sincere. "Say hi to everyone for me."

"Will do."

Still in a daze, she headed back to her car. As she did, another woo-woo moment made the hair on the back of her neck rise and her skin prickle. Could Lacy and Eva be extended family she'd never known about?

Mom, where are you when I need you?

Thrown by the unbelievable news of having a twin—and possibly a triplet—Brynne staggered home, which, since her college days, was above the bookstore. Mom and Rory had wanted to move in together at the house she'd once shared with her mom and Brynne was given her very first apartment—which came with its very own bookstore, no less. Jessica and Rory had used the excuse that it was cheaper to be roommates. She'd suspected what it really meant, but had decided to wait for Mom to tell her. With her illness and death, she'd never gotten the chance.

"You're an independent young woman now," Mom had said. Brynne remembered feeling like an adult for the first time in her life moving into this apartment. Plus, having her mother as landlord meant rent was really cheap.

She entered from the back and stopped on the first landing of the staircase, where the store stairs met up. The route to her apartment was separated by a barrier from customers, which said "Private." Across the walkway was the second story of the bookstore, where special activities also took place. How many people got to call a bookstore their front yard?

She realized the author readings were in progress—*thank you, Rory.* They'd carried on in her absence, and from the looks of it, there was a great turnout. Nate, the bright business major with light umber-colored skin and the most interesting off-center zigzag part in his nearly shaved black hair, probably had a lot to do with the success. He was the one Paul wanted her to give more responsibility to.

Nate glanced up at her on the landing, and as always, his smile was contagious. Another part-time student employee, Arpita Patel, assisted Rory, passing a handout to the attendees. Her long straight black hair curtained her dark brown face, but when her large eyes noticed Brynne, they brightened. Brynne waved at both of them and gave a thumbs-up for their effort, then, pushing through the half door, tiptoed up the stairs to her apartment, unable to deal with one more thing.

Like breaking off her engagement.

Once inside, with the day's events crashing down on her, she dropped her purse on the coffee table and crumpled onto the small living room couch. The weight of her emotions made it hard to breathe.

Curling into the fetal position, she hugged her knees to her chest and finally let out her mixed-up tears. They flowed like a broken dam. What had happened today? She'd broken her engagement, and decisions made in anger were never wise. Tears of sadness. Delivered a baby. Tears of joy. Did she have a relative she'd never known about? If so, was her mother even her mother? Tears of confusion.

After lying in that state, tears puddling on the couch for uncounted minutes, the only thing she wanted was to be held. Only Paul could ground her, but she'd broken things off. Horrible timing. She picked herself up, took a shower, threw on sweatpants and a hoodie, then headed straight to his condo. She wasn't ready to eat humble pie, but she was definitely in need of comfort.

When he opened the door, surprise registered in his eyes, whether because of the way she appeared— she'd looked haunted and a little scared in the mirror at home—or because she'd shown up after she'd broken the engagement. She understood. Her actions were irrational. But some situations were bigger than breakups. She needed him and launched into his arms, holding him tight.

"I knew you'd come around," he managed to say between their frantic kisses. He'd obviously misread her motive.

She stopped, held his face and stared into the eyes she trusted more than anyone else's on earth now that her mother was gone. "I don't want to talk or think right now." She sounded desperate, even to herself. It didn't seem to bother him, though. In fact, from the heated glint in his eyes, he looked ready to deliver on all counts.

Covering his mouth with hers, she kissed him like she'd die if he didn't immediately take her to his bed. He'd obviously just showered, fresh scented from sandalwood soap, hair still damp, like hers. He returned her kisses, opening her mouth and exploring in his familiar way. Exactly what she needed, to forget everything except him. She curled her legs around his waist and he carried her to his room.

With a sigh, she got plopped onto his bed as the strength and weight of him covered her. *Home.* This was her safe place. In his arms, lost in the sensations from his roving fingers and kneading palms, from the flicks of his tongue at the perfect point on her neck and around her breasts.

This she could deal with tonight. Sex. Not marriage or broken engagements. And certainly not the discovery of a person who looked exactly like her.

Later, Paul held Brynne close to his chest, her hair splayed across his shoulders. He kissed the top of her head, smiling at the familiar perfume that was her shampoo, which always made him think of carnations.

Her showing up at his door after her dramatic departure from the restaurant had shocked him. She'd never done it before—just shown up—had always called first. He still cringed at what he'd done, pushing too hard. Forcing her extreme reaction. But, she was here now. One thing he knew for sure with Brynne, even when she was upset, the sex was still great. Always. "Are you ready to tell me what's going on?"

She groaned, fiddling with the patch of hair down the center of his chest, fingers tiptoeing downward for distraction. He stopped her from going further. "What's up? You miss being a delivery nurse?"

Brynne lifted her head, nailed him with narrowed eyes, a how-did-you-know expression.

"Rory called and told me about your heroic delivery at the bookstore. She sounded just as proud as your mother used to." She'd also mentioned something about seeing double.

Her eyes widened as her brows shot up. "I had no choice. That baby was right there."

He squeezed her close again, and her head nestled against his neck and shoulder. "The woman came to the right store." His lips stretched with pride. She remained quiet for several more seconds, and he spent the time feeling her heartbeat synchronize with his.

"You know how I've said I was lonely growing up and pretended I had sisters instead of imaginary friends?"

He nodded, waiting, letting her get around to whatever it was that had made her escape into fiery passion only moments before. Whatever that was had now turned her to reminiscing about forgotten and possibly painful times.

"Like I always felt a part of me was missing?"

"Yes." He gave soothing strokes across her back to encourage her to continue.

"And how I've always insisted I was a loner, an introvert because of being raised in a single-mom household?"

"Go on."

"So, why would I long for sisters?"

"Maybe you're meant to have that big family we've talked about."

"You've talked about," she clarified. "And don't be so full of yourself. I thought we'd agreed to start with one baby and see how it went from there." Though she'd often wondered if Paul or his family had heard and understood that stipulation.

He rubbed her shoulder and cuddled her tight. "We may have gotten a jump on that tonight—you were so impatient, I didn't—"

Up came her head. "Nice try, mister, but you know as well as I do, I'm on the pill. Nothing's happening unless I let it."

He couldn't help but grin. Looking into those amazing blue eyes, feeling her soft, pale skin next to his olive Italian tone, made something stir inside. He loved her so much. All he wanted was to marry her, to be her family.

"And for the record, we're no longer engaged."

He grabbed her buns and squeezed. "That's debatable."

She shook her head. "No. It isn't."

He went quiet, letting her stern response set in. What was the best way to handle this? If they'd really broken up, she wouldn't have come here, and they wouldn't have just gone nuts with each other in the sack. Right? "You used me?"

"The thing is," she said, now up on her elbows, completely ignoring his comment. "The woman I delivered could have been me. It was like staring at myself, except being pregnant." The hair on her arms noticeably stood, and his heart ticked quick beats. Their on-or-off engagement, depending on who said it, had nothing to do with her coming over. Tonight wasn't about him, it was about Brynne.

"Are we entering the twilight zone?"

She nodded in total agreement. "We were identical, and she told me I looked like her twin, Eva, as if I didn't look exactly like *her* already. We didn't have a chance to talk, since Junior was nearly birthing himself on the storeroom floor, but man." She rubbed her forearms, where gooseflesh had popped up. "Her husband was speechless when I went to pick him up. He said it was uncanny how I looked like his wife, Lacy. The woman I'd just helped deliver. He said there was a long story, but he felt it was only right to let Lacy and Eva tell me." She shook her head, obviously still in disbelief.

"What if my mother hid a family from me? Or wasn't even my real mother? She was always so secretive about her past, and she'd never been married—said she never wanted to be. What if she adopted me? She got sick so quickly, we didn't have a chance to talk before she slipped into the coma. No chance for bedside confessions. How will I ever know the whole story?"

"Maybe this woman, Lacy, will clear things up."

"The weirdest thing of all was her middle name."

He offered a confused, questioning glance, content to be her sounding board.

"I saw the medical forms. Her middle name is Taylor." There went the hair on her arms again, and this time he joined her with a whispery chill down his spine.

"That's beyond coincidence," he said. "Definitely twilight zone."

"I know!" She rolled onto her back and covered her face. "I'm not ready to think about all of this." Then rolled back to him. "Make love to me again. Please?"

With that sweet music to his ears, he got over-confident. "Only if we're still engaged."

She huffed and shook her head, letting him know he'd gone too far, then started to sit up and get off the bed.

"Wait, wait, wait!" he said, taking her wrist. "We'll leave that topic aside for now."

Then he held her like he might lose her if he let go, while delivering rough kisses down her neck. His hands roamed her body, pulling her hips tight to his lap. As much as she wanted him tonight, and while feeling closer to her than he had since her mother died, he also suspected that after Brynne had met her double, he'd get put on the back burner again. While all he wanted was to bring her into his family as his wife, now she might be drawn into a potential family of her own. Wouldn't need him anymore. Soon he was as desperate for validation from her as she'd been with him before.

He pushed into her, completely aware of how much she needed him right now, and soon got lost in her welcoming warmth. But one last thought occurred. She'd called his bluff and broken their engagement. He'd have to eat crow, take back that demand, because he could never give her up.

The next morning, after their busy night of running from reality with sex, her cell went off before seven. She left his arms, crossing the room to retrieve it. He immediately missed her warmth and comfort.

Paul watched her, sleek and naked, wavy red hair halfway down her back, hips round and legs thin, pacing back and forth in conversation. Thoughts occurred. First there was her nursing career, then her mother's death and having to switch gears to become a small-business woman, and now a whole new chapter had opened with one, if not two, long-lost sisters?

He loved Brynne, no matter what twists and turns her life would take him through, he wanted to be by her side. Preferably married, but…

Yeah. That was it. First, chuck the ultimatum. Then, get engaged again. After that he'd move ahead with the big surprise.

Chapter Three

After Brynne ended the call, Paul tugged her, with little resistance, into the shower with him. "Who was on the phone?" He pulled her close under the large, square rain head, still wanting to touch her everywhere. Being under warm running water intensified his need to keep her near.

"Lacy. She wants me to come by the hospital so we can talk."

"I'll go with you." They hadn't had a night like last night in a long time. Not since her mother had died. Her demanding his attention solidified how much he loved her. It made him more confident than ever that she loved him, too.

"No, you won't."

"What do you mean? I've gotta see this woman who looks exactly like you."

"We're not engaged anymore."

"Okay, I get it. You're punishing me for giving you an ultimatum. Okay, I remove it. There. Satisfied?"

"We're still not engaged."

He pointed toward the bedroom, through the tiled shower wall. "What do you call all that went on last night?"

"Sex."

"You mean you used me?"

"You see it your way, I'll see it mine."

He took her by the shoulders, slippery with soap. "What's going on?"

She slumped into his arms. "My life is spinning out of control. I need to take a breather."

"From me?"

She nodded.

He stepped out of the shower, reached for a towel and began drying off. "Well, I'm not going to let you go through this alone."

She shook her head, the water running over her hair and face. "Wouldn't it be weird if you didn't think so?"

"You mean, like having a double was all your imagination?" He dried his pits. "Even though her husband and stepdaughter agreed?"

"I know, and so did Rory." She turned to let the water hit her back, watching him through the glass.

"Crazy thoughts. I'm still in denial, having a hard time grasping it."

"I can understand why." She'd just been vulnerable and shared her thoughts, which was unusual for Brynne. If there was a way to support her, he wanted to. "Hey, since it's Sunday, and visiting hours don't start until noon, let's go out for breakfast." Maybe if he pretended things between them were the same as always, they would be.

"You didn't hear me, did you?" Her unhappy expression drove the point home; she wanted to do this on her own. It also proved she meant what she'd said yesterday.

They weren't engaged anymore, and it was his fault. He'd royally screwed up. What if he tried making light of their situation?

He wrapped the towel around his waist then leaned both hands on the shower door. "Then I'm not letting you out of the shower until you take me back."

With her knowing him, that he could never be a bully even if he tried, his move didn't faze her. He could've predicted that. She gave a deliberate head shake, as if he was dense, and worse yet, immature. "Sorry, but we're not engaged anymore, and I think for now that's a good thing."

"So you really meant what you said about just sex? You didn't secretly need my support and comfort?" Which he was hoping meant she wanted to be closer again, the way they'd been when they were planning their wedding.

She nodded, brazen.

Disappointed, he dropped his hands and strode to his bedroom, roughly opening a drawer, pulling out his briefs and slamming it shut. Yeah, he was being immature, but damn it, the woman he loved had once been his to marry, then their dreams began to unravel. Little by little he'd lost Brynne, and all he wanted was to get her back. She appeared behind him, wrapped in a towel, dripping on the carpet. "Look," he said, preempting her from talking first, stepping into his underwear. "If you're serious, then just go."

She stared at him, long and thoughtfully. What he'd give to know what was going on.

"I need to find out who these people are right now. I can't handle anything else."

Which meant he was supposed to be his usual understanding self and just take it. *Okay, Brynne, whatever you say—just yank my chain and I'll follow.* But by his calculations, he was supposed to be married for six months by now. Unfortunately, he was running low on patience. "Can't handle anything else as in the status of our relationship?" His knuckles found his hips, his stance wide.

She didn't wither but stood up to him, naked beneath the towel, looking beautiful. "For right now. Yes."

"So you broke up with me, then came over here

making it crystal clear that you needed me. All night, I might add, and now it's time to drop me, and I'm supposed to be A-OK with that?"

She shook her head in an obvious you-don't-understand-anything way. Was she seriously thinking he was the one being difficult? "I've got to go."

"Well, you better get dressed first," he said, unable to hide his bitter tone. He turned his back to hunt for a shirt. So he'd do what he always did for Brynne, because he loved her. He'd go the extra mile. "And I'm still coming, engaged or not, because you need some backup, and you don't seem to understand that." He yanked open another drawer, retrieved a folded tee, then pushed extra hard to close it.

Retreating to the bathroom, she slammed the door and matched his tone saying, "Fine."

Later, when Paul walked into the hospital room, his step faltered at the sight. "Wow." He sent a quick glance to Brynne. "You've got to be twins."

"Lacy, this is Paul Capriati. Paul, this is Lacy Gardner."

The duplicate of Brynne sat on top of her hospital bed covers in the requisite drab gown with—also hospital-issued—purple no-skid slipper socks. She held a bundle of baby wrapped like a burrito, the only thing showing being a round golden-skinned face with stick-straight copper hair that Lacy had already formed into a faux-hawk. The newborn slept blissfully, his eyelids twitching from the sound of new voices.

Paul had used the hand sanitizer strategically placed by the room entrance and moved to shake her hand, half expecting her to be a hologram.

"I know, crazy, right?" Lacy said, obviously reading his mind, her voice sounding so familiar.

Brynne took a close-up look at the sleeping baby. "Christopher is so beautiful."

First, Lacy dipped her head with thanks. "Zack told you that, right?" Then she cast a suspicious glance at Brynne, an expression Paul had seen hundreds of times, but on Brynne's face.

Brynne nodded, easily giving up her source.

"I told him I want this little guy to be named John, after my dad. He's the one with red hair."

Brynne laughed lightly, obviously not wanting to get involved in the name battle. When Lacy joined in, they sounded identical. The sight of the two of them side by side also knocked some air out of Paul's lungs.

"Maybe you should both sit down." Lacy had clearly noticed his reaction, and he automatically followed her suggestion.

"Where's Zack?" Brynne asked.

"He would've stayed overnight in the room with me, but the hospital doesn't allow kids for that, so he and Emma bunked down at a nearby Best Western."

"I thought you were here visiting family?"

"We were, but they live in St. George. I talked

Zack into bringing me to Cedars in the City, based on a bit of information my brother-in-law uncovered about our adoption."

"Interesting. If you hadn't come here, we never would've met."

"I know." Lacy took a breath, letting the realization sink in. "Anyway, they slept in, and now he's treating her to a special brunch." She glanced at the clock on the wall. "Or maybe I should say lunch, but they should get here soon enough. And this way you and I can get to know each other a little."

Boy, one thing was different about Lacy from Brynne—well, two things. Ask her a question and get a detailed answer, and even though she was holding a baby, it was obvious she liked to use her hands when she talked. Conversation with Brynne often felt like prying open a locked box, and in general, she was a calm talker. Lacy was more like his family—lots of hands and words. Paul helped Brynne find a chair and sit, since she seemed to be slipping back into dumbstruck mode, then sat next to her for support.

"First of all, my twin sister, Eva, is flying in as we speak, so you can meet her, too."

Brynne's hand flew to her forehead. "I don't know if I can handle this."

"If I wasn't so distracted by giving birth yesterday, and now with this little guy—" she grinned down at her baby "—I might feel the same way. Also, after finding my twin, Eva, I'm not nearly as shocked the second time around. Though three is really pushing it." She nearly knocked the water pitcher over on the bedside table with her wide gesture. Paul leaned in to help, but clearly well practiced with hand gestures gone awry, Lacy righted it before it spilled. "I mean, it's still crazy, the situation and all, but whether twins or triplets, or some huge cosmic joke, I'm just happy to have found you." She was a kick to watch talk.

"You honestly think we're related? I've lived here all my life. And you're from?"

"California. I was born and raised in Little River Valley, and Eva, or Evangeline, as her adoption birth certificate says, was raised in Los Angeles." Lacy snapped her fingers, as though beginning to spin a tale of great wonder. "Okay. So, my father and mother couldn't have kids, and they hired a surrogate since my mother was nearing menopause. Like I mentioned, my dad has the red hair, and he donated the sperm." She looked down at the baby. "And that's why we're naming you John, not Christopher, huh sweetie."

"Your parents never told you about the surrogate?" Paul said, curious about every part of this story.

"Never. He died almost two years ago, and I stumbled onto the paperwork in our attic. I'd never been told I was even adopted."

"But he was your father," Brynne added, looking confused.

"Yes, he was *our* father, I'm willing to bet on it. Anyway, my mother adopted me after I was born. That's part of the surrogate process when it isn't your eggs."

Brynne nodded, taking it all in. Paul took her hand and held it, and letting him, she glanced gratefully at him, adding a light squeeze.

See, she did need him here.

"The only reason I was looking for paperwork was because one of my customers at a wedding insisted that I was someone else. Eva, she'd said. Oh, I should tell you I own and operate a food truck, and that's the big trend for weddings these day in Southern California, so that's how that came about."

Paul could tell by the amused smile that piece of information tickled Brynne. She also happened to be a big fan of eating from food trucks, especially the grilled-cheese truck that parked at the university every Friday. A food truck. Huh.

"It was Dad's. The food truck. I had it revamped after he passed away. That's also how I met Zack—I set up at one of his construction sites. The truck is definitely good luck."

Now Brynne smiled full out. Paul could tell she liked this woman, sister or not. Then it occurred to him. "Can triplets be identical?"

That snapped Brynne out of her daze—she obviously gave the idea consideration for a second, as though this aspect of the crazy situation had yet to occur to her. "It's extremely rare, like a million to one, but the fertilized egg has to split twice to get identical triplets. Usually it splits once and the third baby has its own fertilized egg, so they aren't completely identical."

"Well, our egg must have done that. Whatever you just said. Split twice? Here," Lacy said, after picking up her phone from the bedside table and using her thumb to scroll through some pages, Christopher or John still snug in the other arm. "Let me show you a picture of me and Eva." Finding one, which brought a smile to her face, Lacy turned the phone for Brynne and Paul to see.

The wedding picture shot through him like a bolt of electricity. "Uncanny" was all he could manage to say. Still holding Brynne's hand, though tighter now, he rubbed his thumb over her knuckles.

"You guys had a double wedding?" Brynne sounded envious, which was encouraging, and Paul wondered how soon before she'd be lamenting never knowing about family all these years.

"Yes!" Lacy's eyes lit up. "Notice we were wearing the same dress?"

"I did. Different veils, though."

"We didn't pick out that dress together. We each chose it ourselves." There went the free hand again, palm up, stirring the air.

"That's crazy."

"I know." Lacy's expression turned impish. "We played a dirty trick on Zack and Joe, too. When we have more time, I'll tell you all about that, too."

Which made Paul wonder exactly how much time Brynne would have with Lacy and Eva—a day? A week? And then what?

"Well, if I'm not some freak of nature, but actually your sister, we definitely all came from the same egg!"

"Which brings me to ask if you've ever had a DNA test? That was the first thing Eva and I did when we found each other. As expected, we share the same DNA. You should have a test done, right away."

"I will."

"Are Eva's parents alive?" Paul tried his hardest to put this crazy situation into perspective. "Did they give any background on your birth?"

"Eva was adopted by a single mom, and believe me, we've grilled Bridget as much as she'll let us."

"And your parents didn't want both babies?"

Lacy shook her head remorsefully, offering the first glimpse of the emotional cost of splitting up siblings. "Evidently, they couldn't afford two children, so when they found out the surrogate was carrying twins, they didn't know what to do. But the surrogate found another person who wanted to adopt, Eva's mom, so she made twice as much money, or maybe more. Bridget refuses to discuss particulars and insists the adoption was closed and her knowledge was limited."

"That's as far as you got?" Paul couldn't help his curiosity, being a historian, and Brynne being the woman he loved more than anyone, who had probably just found out she was a triplet at the age of thirty-two.

"Bridget let slip a tidbit or two, like she was positive there were only twins, and from that we pieced together the hospital where we were delivered, and a name, so from there we discovered the name of the nurse who'd helped. We actually contacted her, but she wouldn't budge on giving any more information. *Closed adoption*." Lacy exaggerated the words, then performed the old zip-of-the-lips bit. "Though she wouldn't confirm or deny the name we suggested was of the surrogate mother. Which we understand, but sheesh!"

"And you said you were here visiting Zack's family?" Paul continued.

"Yes. They're also from Iron County, but in St. George."

Right, right. She'd already mentioned that, but the emotionally charged information was flying, and it was hard to keep up.

"But I made him bring me here because Eva's husband, Joe, is a lawyer, and he also happens to be the mayor of my hometown." Pride was clear in her voice, and it accompanied the expression on her face. "He did some research and asked a lot of questions, and with Eva's help they found a nonprofit that assists in opening closed adoptions." Lacy stopped, checked out Brynne, as if wondering if she could handle the rest. "When Eva and I both got pregnant, we really wanted to know about our health history. You should also know that Eva has the same middle name as I do. Taylor." She waited for that tidbit to sink in to Brynne. "Your last name." Then she pinned her with an earnest look. "You weren't adopted, were you." It wasn't a question.

Brynne shook her head slowly, but she also shrugged, which under the circumstances seemed appropriate.

Lacy continued. "Joe got us a court date and represented us to a female judge, who was sympathetic to Eva being in her third trimester, and me in the first. She opened the documents for health reasons. The name we discovered as our birth mother was Jessica Taylor, and when we traced her to Utah, we discovered she'd recently died." Lacy went silent, watching Brynne, empathy for the loss pouring from her eyes. "I'm sorry for your loss, but without her consent, we couldn't get the medical history."

Brynne gasped, and Paul went back to rubbing her knuckles, for which she was grateful. With her head spinning from this news, she could hardly put thoughts together. She leaned into him for comfort, and he put his free arm around her shoulder, drawing her closer, his hand soothing her upper arm, up and down. Yes, she was grateful he'd insisted on coming with her, because this information was mind boggling.

"My mother was the surrogate." Brynne needed

to say the obvious aloud, which also proved she was indeed her birth mother, forcing her to swallow the lump in her throat. "She told me she was from California but came here to make a new start. She didn't want me to be raised in a big city."

It was embarrassing how little she actually knew about her mother. Obviously, if Lacy and Eva were her sisters, there was a huge reason her mother kept everything so close.

Lacy and Paul let the silence stretch on as Brynne came to grips with evidence that knocked her sideways. Her heart palpitated and it seemed she was on the verge of an out of body experience. Thankfully Paul anchored her.

"She always insisted she didn't have any family." Brynne stared at the floor, her thoughts flying.

"And I never met my grandparents," she continued. "Mom never spoke about anyone." Brynne's hands flew to her mouth, in prayer fashion, where they rested against her lips as she deepened her thoughts. There was so much she didn't know. Or understand.

"She must've been carrying triplets and gave two away, then thirty-two years ago moved to Cedars in the City." For the first time Lacy sounded solemn.

"I was about to ask why your father and mother allowed twins to be separated, but do you think they knew about a third baby?"

"Bridget, Eva's mom, swears the surrogate only had twins. Evidently they weren't told. It wasn't until Joe got ahold of hospital records that we thought they'd made a mistake stating triplets had been born. Since I was having a baby, and Eva had recently had one, too, we'd hoped to come here to find our birth mother for the health history." Lacy locked her gaze with Brynne's. "Not to find another sister. But then, like I said, we found out she'd died."

Brynne broke into tears, her mother's death being all the more tragic. She leaned forward, and Lacy swung her legs over the bedside then hugged her with one arm while holding the baby with the other. "It's crazy, isn't it?"

The baby's chin quivered, and his eyes popped open, then just as quickly sealed tight again, dropping a huge tender spot in the center of her chest.

"Hopefully, it'll make more sense after the shock wears off," Paul said, in his usual reassuring fashion, though clearly out of his depth. Still, she was glad he'd insisted on coming.

"For the record," Brynne said, "rest assured, Mom was healthy until that crazy virus took her out."

There was a rustle at the door. Brynne assumed it was Zack and Emma, but shaken and emotionally drained her sole focus was on Lacy's sweet and innocent baby. Paul held her and kissed her hair. She didn't fight it.

Lacy glanced in the direction of the door. "Eva!"

Brynne turned and nearly fell out of the chair. Identical sister number three had just walked in.

Chapter Four

Eva burst into the room, and Brynne's lungs shut down. Her heart seemed on the verge of exploding. Eva rushed to the bedside to get a close look at the bundle in Lacy's arms.

"He's beautiful," Eva said, her voice so like Lacy's, who smiled up at her identical twin.

"How could he not be, with Zack as his dad?" came Lacy's wry response. They chuckled knowingly together, then hugged.

For only having met in the last year, they already seemed as though they'd known each other a lifetime, and Brynne felt unreasonably left out.

Dumbstruck, she sat perfectly still, holding on to Paul's hand as though he was her lifeline. And yes, she was glad he was with her. Engaged or not.

Once the initial greeting between sisters ended—sisters who were clearly close to each other—Lacy rolled her eyes in a wide arc to indicate Brynne on the other side of the bed.

Eva followed her lead. "Oh my God." She glanced back to Lacy. "You weren't kidding."

Lacy gave an exaggerated headshake.

Brynne held her breath as another double approached. She thought about rising to meet her, but her legs weren't cooperating, and it would mean having to let go of Paul's hand, which she wasn't ready to do.

"You've given me chills," Eva said, a warm smile on her face. She bent and wrapped her arms around Brynne. "Hello, sister. Long time no see."

Their shared birth date, which Brynne had picked up on from the hospital admission notes, insisted this was true, yet it was still so hard to believe.

The attempt at humor helped Brynne break through her shock. Though the image of sharing a womb with the two redheads was beyond her comprehension. She dropped Paul's hand and reached for Eva's, which rested on her shoulders, once making contact, patting them. "This is all too much for me."

Eva pulled back, empathy in her glassing-up eyes. "Believe me—well, us." Her head tilted in Lacy's direction. "We understand."

Lacy snagged some tissues from the bedside box,

saved one, then handed a couple to Eva, who kept
one and passed the other to Brynne. Contagious as
yawning or laughing, Eva's eyes brimmed. Lacy's
did, too. Overwhelmed by the unfathomable moment, Brynne's eyes pricked and stung. Though a
long-overdue group cry might be in order, they'd
only just met, and each fought valiantly to keep
things under control. Though now Brynne's chin
quivered, driven by confusion and more questions
she'd never get to ask her mother.

What kind of screwed-up history had they shared
without ever knowing until now?

As Brynne, Lacy and Eva recovered from their
initial triplet introduction, Zack and Emma arrived.
"Hey, Eva!" Zack said.

"Hey, yourself," Eva said, in a familiar old-friend
fashion, oddly evoking another envious twinge from
Brynne. "You and my sister do good work."

Zack greeted Eva with a big family-style hug,
as more envy perked up. "Christopher's a little
scrawny, but still beautiful, and Lacy'll get him
fattened up soon enough."

Eva kissed Zack's cheek, while Brynne felt like
a fly on the wall. How must Paul feel? "I have no
doubt. But I thought it was John?"

"Where's Joe?" Zack obviously steered the in-
process baby naming to a new subject, his vote solidly cast.

"In the lobby trying to keep our kids quiet."
More children for Brynne to learn about, more

names, more everything involved with discovering a lost family. It was all too much to take. She didn't want to interrupt but wondered how many more there were and who they belonged to.

"How'd I manage to miss them?"

The hospital lobby wasn't big, but there were corners and alcoves where a dad trying not to make a spectacle of himself could gravitate to. Oh, and the gift shop. There was always something for little ones in there. Mainly candy, but little stuffed toys and books, too. Brynne knew because her bookstore kept that section stocked.

"Good point." Eva grinned at Zack. "Noah is bound to be running around, and Estrella is such a loudmouth. Her cries no doubt are reverberating off the walls as we speak."

Paul jumped up, probably sensing how left out Brynne was beginning to feel, and though at first she'd been annoyed he'd pushed his way in today, she couldn't be more grateful he was there.

"Zack, this is Paul, Brynne's…?" Lacy piped up from the hospital bed.

"Fiancé," Paul said out of habit.

"Ex-fiancé," Brynne corrected, obvious tension returning between her and Paul even after secretly being glad he had come. It also garnered a questioning exchange between the redheads and Zack. But she'd been serious when she'd ended it. He'd pushed her too hard and she'd pushed back. She wasn't nearly as sure about getting married and immediately have babies.

Like a gentleman, Paul ignored the clarification and offered Zack a handshake. Brynne, still in moderate shock, had already failed at hospitality 101 by not beating Lacy to the introduction, but with a great excuse! Still, if she had, the awkward moment could've been avoided. Now word was out, there was tension between her and Paul.

"I know of a nearby park," Paul said, slipping easily into his usual helpful mode. "I'll go find your family and take them there if you'd like," he generously suggested to Eva. Though Brynne wondered if it wasn't to get away after what she'd just said.

"Can I go, too?" Emma, the young girl with thick, wavy hair like her father's, but a shade darker, called out.

"Of course," Paul said to a tween he'd never laid eyes on before, his welcoming, Italian, family-centered roots taking over. The man had no fewer than eight nieces and nephews—he'd know how to deal with Emma.

Brynne could practically read Paul's kind and considerate mind. He must've figured this was one big happy family, but the three sisters could use some getting-to-know-you time, so he'd offered an easy solution. Though Brynne wasn't sure if she wanted to be left alone with these strangers who looked like her.

Zack gave Lacy a quick kiss. "How are you two?"

"We're doing great."

"Should us menfolk clear out?" Zack hiked his thumb over his shoulder.

Lacy kissed him back, then nodded. "Probably a good idea." Christopher—or, to be fair, John, which was still in the running, depending completely on which parent got their way—began crying, and Lacy handed him off to Zack. "He's due for a diaper change. After, can you give him to the nurse for me?" Obviously taking advantage of the hospital setting while she could.

Zack dutifully took his son, grinned at him, then kissed Lacy again, this time goodbye. "We'll be back later," he said. "Paul, wait up for me."

The three sisters sat on Lacy's hospital bed. Brynne still emotionally teetering, and unsure about wanting to delve deeper into this crazy new discovery. All her life, the yearning she'd had for something more, was most likely for her sisters. Could a person instinctively remember all the way back to the womb? Yet now that they'd materialized, she resisted opening the gift.

Lacy and Eva reached over and took Brynne's hands. Something like electricity tickled up her arms when their fingers met. Could they feel it, too?

For several seconds they simply sat in a circle, hands clasped, eyes examining each other up close. It was freaky looking at her own face on two other people. The chills wouldn't stop.

"You've obviously got the best hair," Eva said to Brynne, checking out her long thick braid.

"But your bone structure is the most pronounced," Brynne said to Eva.

"Probably because she eats like a mouse," Lacy broke in.

Eva stuck her tongue out at Lacy, which, coming from such a sophisticated-looking woman, with the blown-out hair and salon style, surprised Brynne.

"Your eyes are the bluest," Brynne told Lacy.

"You think?" Lacy batted her lashes at Eva for confirmation, who, by the tip of her head, agreed with Brynne.

A nurse broke into their mutual admiration society with a freshly changed and swaddled baby. "Wow, Brynne, I really am seeing triple."

"You can only image how I'm feeling," Brynne replied to her former coworker Kris. There was no explaining how she felt both drawn to the possibility of being a triplet and seriously bothered by it being a fact. *I'm used to being by myself.*

Kris handed the baby over to his mother. "He's all yours. Time to nurse." She then made a quick exit, as though she might be asked to do one extra thing if she didn't. Brynne, having worked shifts with her, knew her minimalist style.

After their tight circle got broken up, Eva and Brynne backed away, allowing Lacy room to guide her son's little head as he rooted for her breast.

Normally, meeting a person for the first time,

Brynne was shy, and she felt no different now. They glanced back and forth at each other, each shaking their heads.

"To think you guys were out there all this time" was the only coherent thing Brynne could think to say.

Eva's beautifully made-up face crumpled into tears. "It isn't fair."

In the middle of a chill storm, Brynne felt bad, not meaning to make her cry, yet completely understanding her comment. It wasn't fair, and finding out something like this at this point in her life was beyond baffling. How was she supposed to take it? She couldn't exactly just jump right into having sisters, the way they'd seemed to. Even while knowing without a doubt they were triplets. They were still strangers.

Like a yawn or laughter, Eva's tears were contagious. Soon Brynne joined in. No. It wasn't fair.

"Oh my God, you guys even cry the same!" Lacy said, lightening the mood and helping Brynne and Eva laugh in between their sobs.

"As if you don't!" Eva snarked back when she wiped her eyes, as Lacy's happy tears dripped onto her baby's head.

These women lived in California. They wouldn't be here for long. Knowing that helped ease some of Brynne's mounting anxiety. She should be more excited about meeting them but, once again, her life was getting turned upside down, and she could barely cope as it was.

Finally a lucid thought bubbled up. While they were here, maybe they could unravel more of how they came to be separated at birth, which struck Brynne as a horrible thing to do to babies. "Mom may be dead, but her closest friend in the world, Rory, is like a second mother to me. Maybe she can answer some of our questions."

Paul, amid the noise of kids running and squealing at the large and well-manicured park, noticed Emma taking charge. His guess was she was eleven or twelve, and being the oldest kid on the large composite play unit, it made sense. Currently, she guided Eva's adopted son, Noah, who looked to be around two or three and had jet-black hair, up the climbing section toward the slide exit.

He studied Zack and Joe, the husbands to the long lost sisters. It boggled his mind that these people had been out there in the world all these years without Brynne ever knowing. The men were engaged in friendly, casual conversation, obviously comfortable with being brothers-in-law. Brawny Zack, a fellow Utahn was the owner of a construction company, and was fair haired and broad shouldered. Joe, the Hispanic mayor of Little River Valley, had fashionably groomed black hair and, though he'd just flown in on an early-morning flight, looked photo ready in jeans and a thin crew-necked beige pullover sweater. Though both men were fit, it was obvious Joe was either a runner or a gym regular, whereas Zack's muscles were from a lifetime in construction.

Paul worried he wouldn't measure up in Brynne's mind. Being more bookish, and needing reading glasses to prove it, he did his fair share of workouts and loved being outdoors, but he wasn't nearly as polished as these two from the Golden State. Whatever Brynne's hesitation was about getting married, maybe these guys would add to her list. Still, Paul liked them and wanted to know them all better. He only hoped Brynne would let him come around while they were here.

"Eva told me you're a history professor?" Joe broke the ice.

"Yes, I teach twentieth-century US history, which makes me a World War II geek, I'm afraid."

"I watch a lot of that on cable TV, but Lacy makes me turn it off if she's around."

"Is it politically incorrect to call it a guy thing?" They all chuckled knowingly.

"How long you been at the university?" Joe asked, shifting the little girl with auburn hair from one arm to the other. Judging by Paul's experiences with multiple nieces and nephews, she looked to be six to eight months old.

"Going on six years. I'm hoping to go up for review to become tenured soon, as a matter of fact." Paul had been lucky to snag an assistant professor's job after he got his doctorate in US history.

Soon, after volunteering for every committee he could, he was asked to be the assistant to the department chair.

Now, at thirty-seven, with a solid income and a set timeline to become an associate professor, then professor, he was eager to marry Brynne. Be like these guys. Not because his parents had been nagging him to get married since he'd turned twenty-one, but because he'd finally found the right woman. Now if he could only convince her of that.

"So, you'll be staying here in Utah?" Zack asked.

"Yes. No change in sight for that. If all goes as planned, I expect to become a tenured history professor at the university."

"I guess that means Eva and Lacy will be making a lot of trips up here," Joe said.

"Or we could visit you guys," Paul said, a whole new world suddenly opening in California.

"That'd be great. *Mi casa es su casa.*"

"Same here," Zack agreed.

The men grew quiet again, watching Emma guide Noah on how to go down the tall slide. In Joe's arms, the baby girl named Estrella squealed excitedly. Joe took her to the swings, putting her into an infant seat and giving a gentle push, much to the child's wide-eyed delight.

Zack and Paul stood off to the side, observing the activity.

An earlier passing thought wouldn't quit nagging, so Paul decided to bring it up. "Is it weird?"

He waited for Zack to acknowledge his question. "Being married to Lacy, who looks exactly like Joe's wife?"

"I met Lacy before she'd met Eva, so, I fell for her long before anyone knew she had a twin. Or I should say now, a *triplet*."

Paul shook his head, still baffled at the thought. "I'm trying to wrap my brain around that."

"Me, too! But to answer your question, yes, it is a little strange. The thing is, you know your woman, and that isn't the same as her being Eva's double." Zack looked at his feet for a second, then quietly chuckled. "They tried to trick Joe and me at the wedding. They'd chosen the same dress. Wouldn't let us see the dresses before, because, you know, tradition. Anyway, they switched sides before walking down the aisle. Joe and I are like, wait a second, and we both knew. Immediately. I could tell by the way Lacy walks, and Joe said he could tell by the trendy veil Eva wore, and the fact her baby bump was just starting to come out. Lacy's veil was totally traditional, longer. You know." Zack shrugged, clearly out of his area of expertise when it came to wedding gowns and veils. "Anyway, we knew, and we changed places as they walked up the aisle. They couldn't fool us."

Reassured, Paul thought about Brynne, how he'd swear he'd know her anywhere, even in the dark. Still, it was strange to realize she was a triplet. "Well, we all have excellent taste in women."

"You got that right."

Sensing it was easy to talk to Zack, Paul relaxed. "Brynne and I were supposed to be married last March, but Jessica got sick and died the month before. We've been stalled out on the rescheduling since."

Zack turned to Paul, his green eyes narrowed. "Maybe meeting her happily married sisters will help move things along."

Paul laughed lightly. "A guy can hope."

His ultimatum, as lame and out of place as it had been, only made things worse, and he'd suddenly found himself un-engaged. Brynne had been as excited as he was in January. They'd talked through their individual reservations. How he wanted to start right off with a new place to live, a place they'd call theirs. How she wasn't as sold on making babies immediately as he was. She'd made it clear she wanted to keep working once they had kids, but with Jessica's blessing, they could depend on her for childcare and Brynne had seemed at peace with that. When the unthinkable happened, losing her mother, she'd fallen apart, completely understandable. Now six months later, she was still stalled out on marriage.

He'd done his best to be supportive until yesterday when he'd thrown down the ultimatum. Which blew up in his face. But he'd had her in his arms all last night, knew he loved her and she'd needed him. She may not have said the words outright, but her body language sure was easy to read. They belonged together. He knew it. How much more time did she need?

A hard thought occurred. With two sisters appearing out of nowhere, Brynne had the perfect excuse to be distracted the entire time they were here. He had to make sure he was included, if for nothing more than being her backup. If that meant insinuating himself into every aspect of their visit, he would. He was fighting for a future with the woman he loved, and she'd turned out to be a tough sell.

"Hey, you guys like Italian food?"

They both gave Paul a "who doesn't" look.

"Then you're officially invited to have a meal at my family's home. Would Tuesday night be good?"

"As far as I know, we don't have any plans. Sure," Joe said.

"We'd love to," Zack said, speaking for Emma and Lacy, too.

Step one. Accomplished.

Poor Rory didn't know what hit her when Eva and Brynne walked through the bookstore entrance. She glanced back and forth between them.

Brynne's hair was longer than Eva's, more like Lacy's, but always braided. Eva's came just to her shoulders and required hair products.

"Wait, didn't you—" Rory pointed to Eva "—just have a baby? How are you looking so perfect?" Her eyes zipped over Eva's trim waist before noticing her chic lounging clothes, fit for air travel or a Sunday afternoon entertaining by a pool.

Brynne figured they'd flown first class—she wasn't sure why, just had a strong hunch. She also needed to rescue Rory—who remained clearly baffled. First, she went around the counter and gave her a big hug. "Rory, that was Lacy. This is Eva."

"There's *another* sister?" Rory's incredulous tone made sense to Brynne.

Was she positive yet that Eva and Lacy were her sisters? The fact they all had the same birthday was a major clue. Their middle names of Taylor were another. Truth was, Brynne didn't need a DNA test to prove anything. She already knew in her gut she was a triplet who'd been separated from her sisters at birth. The big question was why?

"Eva, this is Rory, she's kind of like a second mother to me." Brynne gave another squeeze to the obviously confused woman, then explained, "Eva and Lacy are from California, and, as you can tell, they both look amazingly like me." She waited for that information to sink in and watched the color drain from Rory's cheeks. "Did Mom ever tell you about being a surrogate?"

Rory sucked in a breath, then stopped outright. She glanced around at the customers milling around the bookstore, her short black bob shining in the fluorescent lighting, her red glasses reflecting it. "Maybe this isn't the right time or place to have this conversation" was all she said.

Still, it gave Brynne—and, from the obvious glint in her eyes, Eva as well—hope the truth would soon come out. "Okay, agreed, but since we close early on Sundays, will you have dinner with me, Lacy and Eva at the hospital tonight?"

Rory nodded slowly. "Yes. Okay. I'll tell you what I know, but it's not that much." That didn't ring true. Rory had been her mother's closest companion in the world. They'd been roommates for the last ten years. Though they kept separate bedrooms, Brynne suspected how close their relationship might be, but any time she'd had the nerve to bring it up, Mom managed to shut down the conversation. Still, Rory would surely know something about the adoptions.

"Well, whatever you know, it's certainly more than I've ever known," Brynne reminded the woman she'd known as a backup mom all these years. If Jessica couldn't make a track meet, she'd send Rory. If the PTA needed another volunteer, they'd just bring Rory along. Rory had been an honorary member of the family for years, then, as though they'd been waiting for Brynne to grow up, Jessica and Rory had taken a trip to France and everything changed. They'd moved in together, and Brynne had her first apartment.

Unable to hold back the sadness and confusion that swept through her thinking about the past and Mom, and how much to tell her sisters, Brynne needed to clear her throat. And just like that, Eva's hand found hers, giving a quick supportive grip, then letting go.

It was strange and comforting at the same time. But Brynne was used to bearing her burdens alone, and other than Paul, she had rarely let anyone in. Her protective barriers were set like invisible glass. Bulletproof glass. Still, she let Eva hold her hand.

"Jessica trusted me. Swore me to silence."

Brynne reached over the counter for Rory's hand, took it and squeezed. They'd mourned Jessica together, each lifting the other up when one couldn't go on. During the first days and weeks, Brynne wouldn't have survived without her support, and there was no doubt how deep Rory's love for Mom went. Soon, another hand joined in. Brynne glanced at Eva, an outsider, who nodded with reassurance.

Whatever history was going to come out, the three sisters would have to go through it together. Something they should've been doing their entire lives—going through everything together the way they'd started out in the womb—yet...

Whether Brynne wanted to avoid the whole puzzle or not, she was certain she wouldn't have a choice. They wouldn't let her bow out. Not these two who'd been wondering and searching their entire lives. Maybe because Brynne had always had her mom—their mom, too—maybe that was why she wasn't as eager to put all the pieces together. One thing was clear—whether she wanted to or not, Lacy and Eva were on a mission, and Brynne might have to face things about her mother that would change her good memories forever. She wasn't sure she wanted to do that. Plus, it didn't seem fair, now that Mom was dead, to dig up her past when she couldn't speak for herself, but there'd be no stopping her sisters.

Her sisters were realistically complete strangers to her; she hadn't known them all her life. Part of her wondered why she should get to know them now. What was the point? It wasn't like they'd be next-door neighbors; they lived in different states. And they would still be mostly strangers. What would be different now that they all knew each other existed? Why start a relationship now?

Brynne tried to talk herself out of pursuing a personal relationship with her siblings—almost had herself convinced, too. But these strangers, besides looking exactly like her, were both so dang nice, and something else couldn't be denied—they'd all started out in life together. In very close quarters. How could they be strangers?

Brynne watched Paul as they stood in her small living room later that afternoon. He'd stopped by like he always did to pick her up on Sunday afternoons.

Though today was different. Very different.

"I'm sure your parents will understand why I can't come to dinner." Sunday dinner at the Capriati home was as routine as the Rusty Nail on Saturdays.

But that was when they were engaged. Now they weren't. He'd have to be the one to break the news to them, since he was the one with the family. The big family that he never let her forget about.

"They'll probably think I'm making up a whopper of an excuse," he said, understanding as always, his good nature shining through.

"Oh, then, wait," she said, digging out her phone from her hip pocket, finding the selfie of the three Taylor sisters they'd taken earlier, then texting it to him. "Show them that. That'll shut their mouths."

He smiled. "As long as it doesn't give Dad a heart attack."

"Don't even joke." The man had had one for each year she and Paul had been dating.

"Right, but you've got to admit, only seeing is believing on this." He took time to stare deeply into her eyes, which normally thrilled her. But today, the usual sensation fell flat. His were big, beautiful hazel-brown eyes, curtained in thick dark lashes and sloping downward slightly, puppy dog eyes, as Mom used to describe them. They were also called bedroom eyes. Dreamy. Even when he wore glasses, which he was now, they stood out.

She took them off and tucked them in the pocket of his weekend signature—a light denim button-down shirt.

As though hit by a case of amnesia, she took the sweet moment and let her gaze linger on his. Then she did what came naturally with Paul. She kissed him, putting her arms around his neck and leaning against his solid chest as she did.

"We've got some time before I have to go," he whispered over her ear after the kiss.

She'd let anger rule the day yesterday, and it was never wise to make major decisions while angry. Still, she'd run with that anger, adding self-righteousness into the mix, and broken off their extended engagement. Then she'd barreled into the bookstore, fueled on rage, to discover a baby needed to be delivered. That lightning bolt knocked the fury out of her, and ever since she'd questioned the wisdom of breaking up with the best guy in the world.

Just now, she'd conveniently forgotten about the breakup and acted like everything was fine, kissing Paul. He'd followed her lead and propositioned her. What could she expect?

But under the circumstances, with everything that had happened since yesterday, it wasn't fair to Paul, and it felt all wrong to jump in the sack with him again.

Especially after discovering a family she'd never known about—yet another thing to keep her off kilter and fumbling for balance. And here he was offering himself as her escape of choice. Again. Nice try, but this time, it wouldn't work. He was obviously insecure about the invasion of family from nowhere, and taking advantage of her like she'd used him yesterday. Until she figured out what the heck she wanted, whether to be married to Paul or not, she needed to stay strong in her decision.

"We're not engaged anymore, remember?"

Chapter Five

Brynne arrived first at the hospital early that evening, butterflies annoying her stomach. Why did she have to go through this? Change was never easy, but discovering you had sisters at thirty-two was beyond comprehending.

She kept her head down and eyes on the floor as she walked toward Lacy's room, not wanting to engage with people she used to work with, because it was still hard to be here after her mother's death—and now it was extremely odd, under the circumstances of her sisters popping up. One thing was sure—she didn't want to explain the unexplainable repeatedly to her work friends. Fortunately, while walking briskly and holding her breath all the way, she made it to the hospital room without a single social encounter.

When she strolled in, she found Lacy finishing a nursing session. Zack was at her side, complete contentment smoothing the fine lines at the corners of his eyes, creases accentuated by a lifelong tan earned from outdoor construction work.

"Oh. Don't want to interrupt anything."

Lacy screwed up her face and quickly shook her head. "Not at all. If he wasn't such a porker, I'd have been done long ago."

"He's got some weight to catch up on," Zack said, referring to the low birth weight of five and a half pounds.

"Would you like to hold him?" Lacy offered her baby to Brynne. Overwhelmed by a sense of honor—and it being one of those precious golden moments her mother used to insist occurred throughout life—she accepted.

Lacy also gave her a cloth diaper. "He's a spitter. Protect that pretty mauve top."

Zack intercepted his son and helped Brynne place him on her shoulder for burping. Having worked L&D, she knew the drill, and after only a few light pats on his back, the kid let go a sound an adult might make. Which made them all laugh.

"Wow." Zack was impressed.

"We've decided—well, Zack kindly agreed—that John Christopher sounds better than Christopher John, so my dad, the source of our red hair, gets a namesake and top billing."

"So glad you guys worked that out." Brynne tried to keep the swell of emotion from holding her nephew—and that was certainly who he was—to herself. She didn't want to feel it, but it was there. She'd been a paid professional for eight years, yet she'd never experienced this sense of awe when she worked the ward.

As an RN, new life had always been amazing, and it never failed to impress her, but routine was routine, and she'd had duties to perform. The first minutes after delivery were hectic and spent in a rush to clean the newborn, make sure it was warm and breathing, then check the Apgars—on and on went the nurse's list. She'd never had the luxury of time to simply hold a baby, study it, feel its weight in her arms. In John's case, the incredible lightness and fragileness. He was so tiny. And this was wonderful. There was no other word for it. Hmm, maybe there was something to motherhood.

Her chest tightened, and her eyes pricked behind her lids, which was becoming a habit when in the company of this new family. What might it be like to have a baby of her own? What would motherhood look like for her? That stopped her cold. Why did the idea put her on edge? Never had she entertained such a thought before. Sure, Paul was singing the joys of a family, but she'd never visualized it for herself. It'd always seemed his dream, not hers. She'd been a single child with a single mother. Theirs was a quiet life. A life without siblings or men. Aliens, Mom used to joke about men.

She continued to study the perfection of this baby boy in awe. His tiny nose and lips, the eyes squinted tight under the bright lights, the early signs of a cleft in his chin, like his daddy. The obvious copper hair. Maybe there was something to it. She instinctively bounced the bundle in her arms gently and paced, a rocking sway in her steps. Without a thought, she kissed his tiny forehead.

A mistake. A wave of emotion curled through her, nearly making her dizzy.

"The good news is, I'm getting discharged tomorrow morning," Lacy said, thankfully breaking Brynne's disturbing revelations. "The bad news is they want him to stick around another day or two for observation."

"Oh, that'll be hard, but under the circumstances, wise and also routine." Clicking into the nursing role helped Brynne break the spell of potential motherhood and the lure of holding baby John.

"I'll just spend the day here and sleep in one of those chair beds at night until I can take him home."

"Which is something we need to talk about," Zack said.

"Right, yes." Lacy sighed. Obviously the logistics of giving birth ahead of schedule in another city far away from her home was too much to think about with everything else going on.

The idea that they might never have met if Lacy hadn't gone into premature labor sent a shiver through Brynne. Why had it happened that way? As much as Brynne wanted to avoid having made this discovery of sisters, she couldn't deny the meant-to-be overtones. Sheesh and wow. She wasn't prepared to go there.

Eva breezed through the door, carrying several bags, and all their heads turned. The woman had a way of making dramatic entrances just by showing up. "Hello, people, I've got salads, pasta, pizza." The aroma of melted cheese and Italian herbs had made its way to Brynne. Although she was anxious and had a growing kink in her tummy about the evening's meeting, the smell still managed to make her mouth water.

"I've also got good news."

Eva placed the bags on the bedside table, then worked her way over to Brynne. "I've found a huge house to rent for the week, since it isn't ski season yet. Enough bedrooms for all of us, because I'm not leaving my sister and nephew in Utah alone. Or brother-in-law," she quickly added.

Zack screwed up his face as though she'd just hurled an insult.

"Not that it isn't a gorgeous state, Zack and Brynne, but Lacy needs bonding time, not a road trip right off, and heaven knows the bambino is too young to fly."

He took a slow inhale, let it out. "I've been thinking about renting an RV."

Lacy's brows perked up.

"We both know how to drive big rigs." He directed his reasoning to his wife, with her food truck experience. "It's the closest to a home for little Christopher—I mean, *John*, here, when we're ready to make the trip home."

But wouldn't they have to return the RV back *here*?

"Fabulous idea," Eva said. "Joe, the kids and I can caravan with you, driving your car home. But not right away, because *Johnny*—" Eva emphasized the name, since it seemed the debate had finally been settled "—needs to grow some, and we've got a week's rental move-in ready."

"And I'll be sitting tender for several days," Lacy added, Eva and Brynne completely understanding. Though Brynne still wondered about Zack's logistics on the RV rental.

Eva singled out Lacy. "Wait until you see the house. Gorgeous, huge, everything we need, and a master suite with your name on it. So, go," she said to Zack, "check out of that motel and join Joe, the kids and me at the house. There are enough bedrooms for everyone."

A sudden rush of feeling left out took Brynne by surprise. Why should she care? They'd showed up out of the blue and they'd go before she had a chance to bond. Not that she was in any state to bond with anyone right now. Besides, they all lived in California—of course they'd need to make plans to leave, but she'd just met them, and certainly didn't know them. The sudden ache didn't make sense. Considering the mixed up state of her marriage, shouldn't she be happy to get back to normal? Whatever that was…

Though the meeting of triplet sisters was monumental. The sense of loss dug deep, and she snuggled closer to baby John to soothe her confusion, triggering that fear of motherhood instead. Was she even capable? He must have felt her tension and began to fuss.

Eva, being the closest by, responded first. "May I hold him?"

"Of course." Brynne handed the swaddled bundle to her and couldn't help but smile as Eva quietly cooed over the baby. Her gut told her Eva, just like Lacy, was a nice person. Eva was also obviously well-rehearsed from becoming a mother a second time only six months ago herself.

"Oh, he's so gorgeous. Another ginger into the world." She laughed. "Should've known Lacy's hair would dominate your blond." She teased her brother-in-law.

From what Brynne had seen of Eva's baby, Joe's dark hair had blended with hers to create a gorgeous auburn color. Also beautiful. Her thoughts rushed to Paul, wondering what their babies might look like.

Then quickly stomped out the thought. *Wait, I'm not even engaged to him anymore.*

Zack benevolently put up with Eva's teasing and her big plans. He rose to his full six-foot whatever inches, bent and gave Lacy a long and tender kiss, then told her he loved her. How soon would it be for Brynne to miss hearing that from Paul?

Next, Zack sauntered toward Eva, where he placed a gentle kiss on his son's crown. "Daddy loves you," he whispered. He glanced first at Eva, then at Brynne and tipped his head before heading for the door. "I'll leave you to your meeting."

"See you later at the house, and oh—" Eva looked at Brynne. "We're having a big family dinner tomorrow night, so bring your fella, too."

She couldn't very well skip it. "Uh," she started to correct Eva about Paul's "fella" status, but the other two couples came to mind, and the emphasis on "family" dinner, and being odd woman out did, too. Did she want to face all of them alone? And Paul was so great in big family settings. "Okay." Great. How was a girl supposed to stay unengaged?

Zack, continuing to make his exit, may as well have worn a cowboy hat, since that's what Brynne swore she saw when he nodded their way just before he stepped out the door. A gentleman. An outdoorsman. A bighearted guy who loved Lacy with everything he had, tipping his hat on his way out.

Paul might not be an outdoorsman, but he was also a bighearted guy and a true gentleman, and as much as Brynne tried not to think about it, she knew he loved her. If she could only get through to him that his personal timeline couldn't be pushed on her.

Until she understood more clearly why a part of her kept hitting the brakes on marrying Paul—namely the motherhood part—she owed it to herself, and him, not to go through with it.

Maybe it was because in her home, men were completely foreign animals? Or maybe it was because she'd had few close friends growing up, Mom filling in the role as best friend, keeping Brynne mostly to herself. Now she didn't have her for guidance or support. Just a huge hole where she'd used to be.

A crazy thought elbowed its way through all the others—had Mom kept their relationship so tight-knit because of what she'd done, separating her triplets? Maybe guilt had made Mom closer than normal with Brynne.

"Eva runs a small nonprofit and is used to being in charge," Lacy said, this time being the one to pull Brynne out of her ongoing thoughts. "In case you're wondering why she's organizing everything."

Brynne clicked back in, hoping no one had noticed, with a knowing nod. "Got it."

"Yeah, it's like Make a Wish for seniors, except it's called Dreams Come True." Lacy got out of bed and wandered over to inspect the food.

"How neat." She had to admit her birth sisters were both interesting people.

"I love my job." Since baby John was deeply asleep, Eva gave him back to Lacy, who received him with stars in her eyes. It was the look Brynne had seen countless times working L&D but had never truly grasped until meeting Lacy and delivering her baby. The boy was linked to her by DNA, not to mention would forever be her first single-handed delivery, and those two elements made all the difference. Brynne had felt her first twinge of maternal instinct because of that.

"You seem to know everyone around here, yet you work at the bookstore?" Eva said.

"I inherited it from Mom, and it's my way of honoring her, running the store instead of selling it."

"You seem such a natural at nursing. Do you miss it?"

"I do, but I grew up in that bookstore, and I love supplying avid readers with their drug of choice. It may not be what I was educated and trained for, but the store belongs to me now," Brynne said, surprised by how resigned she sounded.

A quiet presence stood at the doorway drawing her attention. Rory, the woman of the hour, who also held second-mom status, had arrived in her usual work clothes—tailored shirt, black pants, red vest and bright red sneakers, red Harry Potter frames.

After introductions and Lacy proudly showing John to Rory, Eva wasted no time pointedly mov-

ing the conversation along. "What can you tell us
about Jessica Taylor?"

It struck Brynne as unnecessarily abrupt. Rory
had worked all day—Brynne had asked her to cover
her normal Sunday shift—and come straight to the
hospital. From her appearance, she hadn't touched
up her makeup, and her hair needed a brushing. Her
glasses matched the vest she wore at work, with
her name tag still in place. She'd forgotten to take
both off.

Brynne put her hand on the back of Rory's shoulder. "Thank you for coming," then gave her a hug
before searching for a place she could sit. She also
cast a sideways questioning glance at Eva who
caught on and thoughtfully moved a chair behind
Rory's knees then helped her get comfortable.

"Apologies," Eva said, "It's the circumstances of
our birth, and I was a little too focused, just then."

Looking on the hot seat, Rory tipped her head
as if understanding.

"I'm Lacy, and you met me Saturday," she said
far more hospitably than her sister, perching on the
edge of the hospital bed. "Are you hungry? I am,
and Eva brought some great-smelling food."

"Right," Eva said, "Sorry about that. Shall we eat
first?" Taking the helm as hostess, Eva handed out
paper plates, dished salads and pasta onto them, and
passed out loaded vegetable pizza. As their mouths
filled and the questions simmered, at least their ap-
petites got appeased. Though Brynne's hunger was

iffy at best, she still managed to eat a little. In between bites, they chatted superficially about Utah weather and the bookstore. Lacy loved mysteries and Eva women's fiction. Rory's was fantasy, and Harry Potter all the way. No surprises there.

"Brynne tells us you were our mother's best friend," Lacy said, the first to finish her slice and lick her fingers.

It was clear Rory was still having a hard time processing the appearance of two more Brynnes. She'd hardly touched her food.

"Anything you can tell us will be greatly appreciated," Lacy went on.

"Did our birth mother ever tell you she'd been a surrogate?" Eva got to the point.

Rory smoothed out an imaginary wrinkle in her polyester pants as she thought. "Surrogate pregnancies were illegal in Utah until 2005, when a new law legalized them. Of course, Jessica moved here in '91 from California, but she never brought up the surrogacy until we'd been friends for ages—at least five years. She'd just said she'd done it and it'd helped her buy the bookstore, then she didn't bring it up again for almost ten years, until right around the time the new law made it legal here."

The relevance made sense, but how could her mother's closest companion not know the whole story? Just how closed off was Mom?

The triplets sat silent, the only sounds coming from John, who squirmed, yawned and tried to open his eyes, then went immediately back to sleep. Everyone watched as Lacy put him in the bedside drawer, set up like a bassinet for the newborn. Brynne's mind was spinning too quickly to try to do the math Rory had just laid out. When Lacy closed the bedside drawer, Brynne knew it went through to the nurses' side for newborn care.

"She told me she'd been paid to have a baby in California and that money had helped her begin a new life."

"What else did she say? Did you ask questions?" Eva leaned forward, eager for more, ready to take the lead on this meeting.

"She never gave me the details—just said she'd done it. It felt like a confession, and I didn't want to betray our friendship, so I thought it best to let her tell me what she needed to and to not be over inquisitive about the rest, out of respect." Brynne wondered if that was a hint for Eva.

"So that was it? You let the topic drop?" Eva said, obviously not picking up on it, with a touch of frustration in her tone.

"She certainly never said anything about triplets. I'd assumed the surrogate baby was a separate pregnancy from Brynne, though Jessica never told me about being involved with anyone."

"Did she ever talk about her parents? Her family?" Lacy asked.

"Rarely. Just said she'd been born in the San Fernando Valley in California, was raised there and never wanted to go back. Oh, and said she didn't get along with her parents."

Brynne knew that part since that had always been the reason her mother had given as to why they'd never exchanged Christmas cards, or whenever she'd asked about her grandparents. She never remembered getting so much as a birthday card from them, either. When Brynne had asked about her other grandparents, since some of her friends had two sets, her mother had flatly said they didn't exist. *How could that be? Were they dead?* she'd asked, and all her mother had done was shrug. When she'd made the mistake of asking who her father was, all she got was a long dead stare. "Someday, maybe," Mom had said, "but not now." *Something is very different about my birth*, Brynne remembered thinking as a thirteen-year-old. She'd gotten such a negative reaction from Mom, she'd never broached the subject again.

Yet they did get a card from someone named Allison every year, an aunt Allison, who lived in California. A huge state. Why hadn't Brynne been more inquisitive? Probably because of the off-limits response she got asking about grandparents. Her mother had clearly cut herself off from her past, and Brynne hadn't wanted to keep bringing it up. Of course she'd had no clue she was a triplet then!

For the first time, she acknowledged her self-centeredness in her teens, and it stung. If she'd just cared more about her history back then, maybe they all wouldn't be scrambling for parts of a puzzle that was woefully short on pieces now.

"No sisters or brothers?"

Rory shook her head. "Not that I knew of. She never talked about anyone back home."

"She just said she'd been a surrogate mother and that was it?"

"Like I said, she was a private person, and the only reason that came up was because we were talking about the new Utah law going through. I think she thought she'd shock me, but she didn't. I loved her anyway. After that I shared some of my past, which I don't care to discuss with you all, if you don't mind."

"We understand," Brynne was quick to say. Rory had been a dear family friend all her life, her mother's housemate for the last ten years, and she didn't want to forfeit that now with her mother's passing. She'd taken the death as hard as Brynne had, and they'd bonded like never before as they mourned her together.

"I remember wondering if the surrogate pregnancy was before or after little Brynne had been born. But she never pinned down the dates and, like I said, on that one detail, I didn't pry."

"Wait," Eva quickly responded. "What do you mean before or after Brynne? Didn't she show up here with a newborn?" Obviously less invested in Brynne's mother, Eva's mind was quick and sharp, wanting desperately to get information.

Rory removed her glasses and rubbed her eyes

as she thought. Dark circles hung beneath them. A cloisonné ring that matched one Jessica had worn around her neck on a chain. "No. Brynne was around three when Jessica moved here. I mentioned they'd moved here in 1991."

Evidently no one had done the math. Brynne certainly hadn't tried.

"Three?" all three sisters repeated together.

"Then where did she go after she gave birth?" Lacy was the first to formulate the shared thought.

"The records pointed to Utah," Eva added, totally perplexed.

Rory shook her head. "Jessica and Brynne moved into the apartment next to me when she was three. I clearly remember, because this little redhead held up three fingers and told me she was *fwee* the instant Jessica introduced us." For the first time since she'd stepped into the hospital, Rory broke the tension with a smile. "You said your auntie had given you the white polar bear you were holding for your birthday."

Auntie? Auntie Allison, who I don't remember?

"But you said Jessica didn't have sisters or brothers." Eva looked as confused as Brynne felt with no clear memory of what Rory spoke about. Just a vague image of sleeping in a different bedroom.

"Right. But Jessica had an aunt, not Brynne. I never met her or heard anything else about her. I just remember that first meeting with little Brynnie." Rory glanced fondly at her, and if she hadn't been so turned inside out with pieces of memories and questions in need of answers, Brynne would've given her another hug.

Several moments passed in silence as things sank in. The sisters glanced at each other, mouths shut, thoughts practically crawling out of their ears, yet no one said a word.

"You and Mom were inseparable," Brynne said. "It's so hard to believe you don't know more."

Rory glanced at her paper plate of food, still well over half-full. She found the bedside trash can and dropped the remains inside. "Your mother meant the world to me, you know that, and I never want to betray her trust."

"Does that mean you know stuff but won't tell us?" Eva asked, and the hard push bothered Brynne. Was it necessary?

Rory shook her head. "It means I'm telling you all I know about Jessica being a surrogate."

"But she died, and we have some legitimate questions," Lacy politely broke in. "Surely you understand that."

"Yes. I can only imagine finding out you're triplets. It's been a tough several months. Let me have some time to think. See if I can make some sense of what Jessica told me and what I'm seeing in front of me now."

Rory was clearly holding something back, but who could blame her under the circumstances? Two of the three people who looked alike were strangers to her. Was the silence to protect Jessica or herself?

Brynne would never want to force Rory to say anything. She and Rory had grieved desperately together when Mom had died. They'd both loved her deeply. She'd never want to forfeit their friendship, even over the truth about being separated from her sisters at birth. But the big question remained—what could drive a young woman to do such a thing?

"Can you do us a favor, Rory? I know we both packed up Mom's stuff. You kept some, I stored some. Can you go through that again and see if you come up with anything significant?"

"Of course," Rory said.

Something was clear—Brynne needed Paul again. Not to drag him into her bed to help her forget the avalanche of information, emotions and thoughts pounding down on her. Not this time. This time she needed him for his attic, and to retrieve those stored boxes of her mother's personal effects since her apartment had zero storage space. Surely there would be something connecting Mom to an aunt. Maybe they'd come up with something to help figure out where she had been for those three unaccounted-for years after the surrogate births.

Brynne sought out first Eva's gaze, then Lacy's. "I think I've got a plan B."

Chapter Six

Brynne followed Rory out of the hospital room, leaving Lacy and Eva chatting inside. "May I ask another huge favor, Rory?"

The dark-haired, middle-aged woman adjusted her glasses. "Of course."

"While Lacy and Eva are here this week, I'd like to take some time off."

"Absolutely. You need to spend as much time as possible with them. I'll arrange for Nate and Arpita to pick up extra shifts, and the new hire would probably like to get some extra hours, too."

"Great. Thanks so much." She hugged Rory goodbye after reminding her to look for old cards or letters from Aunt Allison in Jessica's stored boxes of belongings at home. Then promised to do the same. Once she'd seen Rory off at the elevator, she made a call to Paul.

"Hey, this is a surprise," he said. "How's it going?"

"Well, we haven't solved any major questions, but we're working on a new lead."

"Good."

Engaged or not, they'd slipped into a comfortable pattern. She suspected Paul didn't believe they weren't actually engaged anymore. Was she positive herself? "How'd your mom take my no-show?"

"When I explained what was going on, she and Dad were amazed and can't wait to meet your sisters. In fact, I kind of already invited Zack and Joe and everybody for dinner there Tuesday."

"You what?" This was part of the problem, being taken for granted. And how was that supposed to work, anyway? Nope, she needed to put a stop to that one big happy family notion. "Not a good idea."

"Why not?"

"You should have asked me first, and, we're not engaged anymore!"

He sighed, long and slow. "Well, I blew it, and they already accepted."

"You have to cancel."

"Won't do that."

Of course he wouldn't. He was a Capriati. They loved entertaining—something completely foreign to Brynne, to the point of being borderline weird. This was part of what steamed her, he expected her to be like him, outgoing, friendly, normal! She should be happy to have someone willing to host the out-of-town guests. They'd quickly discover what a social dud she was otherwise. But under the circumstances, being forced by Paul issuing that ultimatum, it really was crazy. Though what, over the last two days, hadn't been?

Silence stretched out the seconds. "You called for a reason?" he finally said.

Everything was complicated, and would only become more so. She didn't have a fighting chance unless she focused on one thing at a time. And now it was digging deeper into her mother's past. "I need to stop by later—"

"You're wearing me out, but I'm not complaining." As expected, his mind went directly to her showing up in need of consolation yesterday, which had landed them in his bed.

"Not for that." Admittedly, the distraction still held appeal. "I stored some of my mother's boxes in your attic, and I need to go through them tonight."

"I'll be leaving my parents' house within the hour, then I'll look around and get them down for you."

"Thanks! They should be labeled. See you later. I'll text when I leave the hospital."

"I love you." He never skipped an opportunity to tell her. Even now.

Her usual response was "I love you, too," but this time she clamped her lips shut. Her silence must have been painful for him, but she needed to make the point—things were different now.

"I just wanted to bring up what I said yesterday at the Rusty Nail." Her silence had obviously rattled him.

"The ultimatum? Seriously? That's what got us un-engaged!"

"But Brynne, what better time to get re-engaged than when your new family is here?"

Every muscle tensed. How much more could she handle? Her jaw muscles nearly cramped. If he were in front of her, she might try to strangle him.

"Something tells me if I don't make my stand now, I may never get another chance." He qualified, but she wasn't buying.

"Number one, you're being manipulative, which isn't like you. Number two, this isn't the time to have this discussion," she blurted, pinching her brows, though something way in the back of her mind agreed with him. She'd broken up with him because he'd gotten too pushy during a tough patch in her life. He was supposed to be on her side. The problem was he wasn't letting her run and hide. And, now, neither were her sisters!

She shook her head, wanting to pull her hair out.

"Okay, you're right. I'm sorry."

He had to know how angry this made her. He loved her, still wanted to marry her. Did he not get it? Oh, wait, he'd just apologized and agreed with her. "Okay then."

"As a sincere apology, I'd like to suggest you do a little blow-off steam shopping. Why don't you buy something for yourself on me?"

She shook her head. Go shopping now? Was he insane? "Like I have time?" She chose a diplomatic reply, though spoken nothing like a diplomat.

"Who doesn't have time on the internet? Maybe it will help relax you a little, because I'm getting worn out doing the job."

She knew he was teasing, trying desperately to lighten the mood, still she wanted to slug him.

Wait a second, it could be a form of retaliation, to teach him a lesson. She could buy an outrageously expensive dress on his dime, of course never intending to keep it, just to make a point. Don't push me! Then maybe he'd understand how angry she was. But, in her usual style, she held her honest reaction inside. "I'll see if I have time. You may be right about it helping me get my mind off everything."

"Good, so let me give you my credit card number. And I'm serious, get anything you want."

"Ha! Giving me your credit card number. You really are crazy."

"Only about you. Got a pen? Ready?"

Oh, she was ready, all right. The guy didn't know what he and his credit card were in for. Once she'd found a pen in her purse, he recited the card numbers, and she wrote them on her palm.

"Okay, then. Thanks." The least she could do was be polite before she plotted her revenge. "I better go."

"Have fun shopping."

"Oh, I will…" It came out like a threat. Maybe she'd buy two dresses—one for the ultimatum and one for inviting everyone to dinner at his house without asking her first.

"I'm serious, have fun and buy something special." Did he think he could buy her back? Who was this man?

"Like I said, only if I have time." She disconnected her phone, put it in her hip pocket and headed back to Lacy's new-mom suite.

When she got there, both Eva and Lacy were finishing up texting. Probably with their husbands and kids. Brynne felt out of the loop. Their loop.

Rather than leave the hospital right away, since Eva showed no sign of planning to go, Brynne stuck around, too. The draw of more getting to know you time alone with her sisters was too great to resist. Lacy had on street clothes, and once the nurse took little Johnny for his bath and evening weight check, she made her idea clear. "Let's take a walk. I'm going stir-crazy."

"Sure." Eva seemed eager to stretch her legs, too.

"Fine with me," Brynne said, knowing the hospital as only an employee could.

They stepped out of the hospital room, which

was one of sixteen on the ward, making their first public appearance as triplets, and heads turned. It was odd to get so much attention for doing nothing at all. Fellow nurses and visitors alike smiled. Some mouthed "Wow," while others just stood there looking at them.

Being the center of attention had never been Brynne's thing, or her mom's, but being a triplet sure changed that. It was a price she'd never had to pay before now. For the next week, she'd just have to get used to it. Then things would go back to normal.

"Want to go to the cafeteria or the lobby?" she asked. "Someone might still be playing the piano there, though. Might make it hard to talk since the acoustics are awesome." And heaven knew they had a lot of subjects to catch up on.

"Cafeteria," Lacy piped up.

Brynne checked her watch—the cafeteria would be closed by now, but sodas, coffee or tea, a few refrigerated items and packaged goodies would still be available. It would also be free of hospital employees and staff, making it a nice quiet place to talk. With lots of tables to choose from. After her short phone conversation, she wondered about Paul as she pushed the down button at the elevator. Could she really walk away from everything they had together? The tiny ball of anxiety she carried daily lately grew exponentially for a second then subsided. Her palms tingled in the aftermath.

"How long did you work here?" Eva asked as

they entered single file into the box-size, space leaving the Women and Newborns Unit behind.

"Eight years." For the rest of the four-story ride, Brynne, forced once again to be the center of attention, gave a nutshell version of her work as an L&D nurse. To her surprise, both Lacy and Eva seemed fascinated.

Once the elevator doors opened and they stepped out, it was Brynne's turn to make a request. "You guys need to tell me all about your jobs and—" she glanced between her sisters "—what you've been up to the last thirty-two years."

They laughed ironically at the huge task and walked toward the flashy new cafeteria, where the half-moon-shaped salad bar was indeed closed and the room, as predicted, was nearly empty except for some stragglers.

"Got a week?" Eva said, a hint of sadness in her perfectly made-up eyes.

"I know, right?" Lacy said.

"Well, you guys *are* here for the next week." Brynne wasn't sure how she felt about that. Was a week too much, or would it turn out not to be nearly enough?

"True," Lacy said as she spied a piece of pie in the refrigerator section, then went for it.

The next few minutes were spent making decisions on what unnecessary food or dessert item they did or didn't need, ordering various coffees from the one remaining cashier, and finding a quiet corner to claim as their own, away from the six other people there. Once settled in, after Brynne's first sip of machine-made café au lait, they were all ready to get back on topic.

"What's your take on Rory and your mom?" Lacy asked, after her first taste of banana cream pie.

"She was Mom's best friend, and they confided in each other as long as I can remember. I'm shocked if Rory doesn't really know the whole story about the surrogacy."

"Well, she can't help if your mom kept the truth from her." Eva said, sticking a pretzel into a small container of hummus. "The question is why?"

"Maybe if word got out that Brynne was a surrogate baby, some judgy types might say something?" Lacy commented.

"Fair point. I remember having a tough time in elementary school. Though surrogacy was not a big topic on the playground." Brynne was surprised she'd made a joke, and they'd both laughed over it. But she couldn't wait to ask the next question, which was completely random. "Did you guys used to get teased just for having red hair?"

Eva shook her head no.

Lacy tilted hers in thought. "Maybe once or twice, but everyone knew my dad was the food truck guy—he had red hair, and they loved his cooking, so I mostly made out like a star." She glanced at her sisters as she took another bite of pie and swooned like it was to die for. Though the inviting bananas-and-cream scent made Brynne's mouth water, Lacy didn't offer either of them a taste as proof. "You know, small town, not much to make over." Her noneating hand gestured in swirls.

As they settled in, Eva curiously watched Brynne. "Tell us about Paul. Why haven't you guys rescheduled your wedding yet?"

Brynne sighed. How could she explain the latest update on their plans? "We're not engaged anymore." She waited and let the statement sink in. Because of the way she'd been Velcro-ed to his hip earlier, they both looked puzzled.

"Paul's a great guy. I'm pretty sure you can tell."

Lacy and Eva bobbed their heads in agreement, obviously ready for more information. Information she hated to break to them.

"He's a good man, but he blew it yesterday." She fiddled with the rim of her thick mug, the strong coffee aroma promising to taste great. "He gave me an ultimatum."

That got their attention. Lacy jerked her head up and tore her gaze from scraping up the last of her pie with her fork. Eva pulled in her chin.

"Yeah. We either get married now, or he's done waiting around."

"That's harsh," Lacy said.

"The man's frustrated," Eva clarified. "Like Brynne said."

"He knows I'm hesitating, and I think he's worried I don't love him. Needs me to prove it. So he pushed too hard, and I made a brash decision out of anger. But I've got to be honest, having Mom die with zero warning knocked the wind out of me. Rory's been wonderful, but the only other person I've ever loved as much as her is Paul. I know it's irrational, but what if I lost him, too?" Wow, this was a revelation she hadn't realized until her sisters prodded her to talk about him. And it was easy to talk to them—kind of like talking to herself.

"You're obviously still in grieving mode, because the odds of Paul getting sick or dropping dead are nil. He's a healthy man, unless he has some rare disease you haven't told us about."

"No, you're right, he's healthy as an ox," Brynne said, flashing on exactly how healthy he was, especially this weekend, when she'd been so needy, and he'd done a whole lot of...proving.

"To be fair, her mother was probably in good health, too," Eva said. "But that killer virus must have been a freaky fluke."

"She was." Brynne hung her head at the mention of her mother's last few days fighting for her life and losing.

"That's why you're protecting yourself," Lacy said, getting back on point.

"Partly." She wasn't ready to talk about the issue of kids, and the need to negotiate how many, and on whose timeline, when even one seemed overwhelming without her mother around as backup.

"He's got a huge family, and I was raised with

just Mom. There was never a man in the picture growing up. I have no idea how to live with one."

"He'll teach you," Lacy said, sweetly, consoling with her reassuring smile.

Hoping for some backup, Brynne wasn't sure how to respond. And where did these two get off acting like they were long and trusted family members, when they'd only just met each other? Yeah, she was getting defensive, as she'd expected from the start.

"Just make sure you teach him how to live with you, too. That's how marriages work," Eva wasted no time adding. Brynne had quickly figured out who of the three was the pragmatist.

They made it sound so easy, promising to love and honor someone for the rest of your life, then actually being expected to do it. Mom never had. Rory had been married for ten years and was a new divorcée when they'd moved to Cedars in the City, but she'd never had another boyfriend that Brynne knew of. Proving lots of marriages were failures. Were her mom and Rory happy without men? They certainly seemed to be.

But Eva and Lacy seemed ecstatic with their husbands and babies, and being honest, Brynne felt a tugging in her chest since being around them. *I want what they're having.* But she'd put a stop to all that yesterday.

"I guess I should tell you one more thing." She had their undivided attention, but she still waited a moment to say the rest, knowing how disappointed they'd be. In her? Why should she care, right? For the record, they still qualified as strangers. Yet she already did care. Turned out coming from the same womb changed everything. "I broke it off."

"The engagement?" they said in unison.

She nodded, avoiding their stares. "It wasn't just the ultimatum. Or my not knowing how to live with a man. He wants a big family, and well, babies are my job. Not my passion. We're not compatible."

A warm hand found Brynne's forearm and squeezed. Eva.

Brynne had gone inward, deep in thought, often her favorite place to hang out. It was also a place Paul had to coax her out of from time to time. Like the day he'd asked her to set the date all over again. As in ASAP. The day she'd stumbled through excuses for putting it off. Again. For the first time, she'd been honest enough with herself, and now her sisters, to admit why. The big family was the deal breaker.

"And you've got the bookstore now," Eva added. "That's completely different."

Brynne nodded, knowing her heart wasn't in the bookstore. Not like her mother's was. "I call what I'm doing honoring my mother, but most of the time it feels more like an obligation." She'd inherited the store. She wanted to be noble, she did, but… "My heart is in nursing."

"So why not go back to it?" Lacy asked.

"Nothing seems that easy."

"Understood," Eva said empathetically.

They chose silence for the next few seconds, since it was obvious they couldn't solve Brynne's issue over coffee. And truth was, they barely knew each other. After everyone was just about finished, Lacy popped up with a new topic.

"Had you gotten as far as choosing a dress before your mother fell ill?"

At least this one had potential for fun. Brynne glanced at her palm and the credit card number. "It feels so strange calling her your mother when she's our birth mother, too," Eva added.

"Yeah, I guess you're right, and everything *is* a little confusing with us," Brynne agreed, trying her best to stay out of her head and pull herself back into the conversation. "But to your question, I had picked out a dress for the wedding."

"Do you have a picture?" Lacy pushed her plate away, making a hopeful expression.

"Probably." Brynne dutifully brought out her cell phone, scrolled through some websites, then entered a line name and specific style. "Here."

She showed them the wedding dress. A simple white, off-the-shoulder portrait-style neckline and a mermaid fitted bodice, which hugged to the hips then flared from the knees down. A beautiful dress meant for a better time in her life. One when she'd thought she also wanted Paul's dreams.

"Oh my God, that's gorgeous," Eva said as she looked at Brynne approvingly.

"But you didn't buy it?"

She shook her head. "It was on order, but we cancelled. It's for a spring wedding anyway."

"True, but you've got great taste." Coming from Eva, who appeared to be a fashion plate, the compliment felt great.

"And like I said, we're not getting married anymore."

"But *what if* you were still getting married?" Lacy went for the cockeyed-optimist award. "What kind of dress would you buy for that?"

Only because they were who they were, and Brynne needed to try to be hospitable, she decided to go along with their line of conversation. She could play what-if, as long as it stayed a game, because there was no what-if about her decision to put their wedding on hold. "He wanted to elope. I wouldn't have a clue what to wear for that."

"Elope?" Lacy blurted.

"To Vegas."

"To Vegas?" Eva repeated, excitement in her tone. "We're caravanning down that way next week. Why not go with us and we can all be there for you?"

Brynne's chest tightened at the suggestion. "Did you guys not hear me?"

They tossed a guilty look back and forth.

"Sorry," they said in unison, making Brynne feel like a party pooper.

"Totally out of line, expecting you to get married for our convenience. Serious apologies," Eva continued, reaching for Brynne's hand and squeezing.

"Well, if we ever reschedule, I'll expect you two to come."

"We'd love that!"

"But on your own time."

"Thank you. The idea of getting married scares me enough, but the thought of rushing into something that's supposed to last a lifetime freaks me out." She'd kept those feelings at bay while they'd first made plans after getting engaged eighteen months ago, taking one step at a time. Hoping she'd change and see how wonderful the idea was as they went along. They'd even worked out the main issue about having one kid versus a batch of kids. She'd try motherhood out one baby at a time, no guarantees for more, and with her mother's help, it seemed doable. "But this *elope or else* approach Paul threw at me yesterday put everything on a hyperspeed," making her want to slam on the brakes even harder.

"He's got this—" Brynne started with her "Paul's big family" description.

"Big family, yeah, you've mentioned it a time or three," Eva cut in.

"And they'd kill me if we eloped."

"No, they wouldn't," Lacy said, looking appalled. "They'd understand."

"But you don't know them," Brynne sounded like she felt. Defensive.

"I suspect they've raised a decent son, or why would you get engaged to him in the first place," Eva continued. "And under the circumstances of Jessica dying and having to cancel the original wedding, how could his parents not understand?"

Brynne's hands flew to her cheeks, her fingers sliding over her lips until they met in a prayer pose, thumbs latched under her chin as she thought.

A stupid little voice from way, way back made a suggestion. It ticked her off as much as Paul suggesting they elope ASAP. Wasn't it time to have a long talk with Paul again about all of her concerns, and especially about motherhood and reinforcing the baby option now that Mom, her backup, was gone? Meanwhile, her new sisters sat staring at her, so she felt compelled to say something. Anything! "But I don't have a dress?"

Eva and Lacy looked at each other and blurted laughter. Brynne had to join in, knowing how lame she sounded.

"First off, you can wear anything for a courthouse wedding, if that's how you want to go in Las Vegas," Eva said, and trusting her knowledge of style completely, Brynne believed her.

"He did happen to give me his credit card number tonight. Said I could buy myself anything I wanted."

"This guy sounds like a dream!" Lacy said, grinning. She grabbed her phone and started punching and poking it until a backyard-bride website popped up featuring simple dresses for simple weddings. There were dozens and dozens to choose from, and the sisters spent the next hour narrowing down the choices until they all agreed on one. A short, white, V-neck sheath with overlying blouson bodice covered in swirling beads and sequins for a wholesale song. If she'd plotted revenge with this dress, it would hardly make her point. No budget breaker, yet classy and cute. Best of all, it came in an off-the-rack size that Brynne knew would fit.

"You can show off your legs with this one," Eva said. "Did your mom have good legs?"

"Or did we get them from Dad?" Lacy chimed in, acknowledging what Brynne had kind of thought about herself but never dared verbalize, until Paul had informed her early on in their dating that without a doubt, she had a great pair of legs.

Wouldn't buying a wedding type dress and not just any old expensive-as-hell dress to get even send the wrong message? "This doesn't have to be a wedding dress, right? I can wear it for other occasions."

"Absolutely," Eva assured.

"As if I ever go to parties."

"Hey you never know. Plus the holidays are right around the corner," Lacy said.

"Should I?"

"Wait," Eva said. "Can they deliver in two, three

days tops? Since we helped pick it out, we'd love to see it on you while we're here."

Lacy moved the website information around on her phone screen until she'd located the shipping information. "Yes!"

Brynne glanced at her sisters, who'd somehow hijacked her revenge shopping, increasing her anxiety, but in an odd way, also giving her courage. She gave a crazy mixed-up nod. "Let's do it." More in the vein of "whatever" than "I'm going to make this great payback decision hurt."

With that Lacy ordered the dress, and when the time came, Brynne read Paul's credit card numbers, which had started to blur thanks to her hands going clammy.

"There's all the proof I need to know that Paul is perfect husband material," Eva teased, noticeably impressed with his trust and generosity.

Despite the hesitation, Brynne admitted to being excited about the purchase; she couldn't wait to try it on. Lacy started it, once she'd pushed "Submit," then they all joined in and squealed together. Completely out of character for Brynne, who'd never been a squealer. But it felt kind of good.

"What'd we just do?" Brynne blurted.

"I don't know, but it sure was fun," Lacy said.

"We bought you a chic dress paid for by a good guy named Paul, who, in case you've forgotten, wants to marry you," Eva said.

Whose team was she on?

"Will Lacy Gardner please return to her room?" came over the hospital paging system the moment they'd completed the transaction.

"Oops," Brynne, said, knowing well there was a 9:00 p.m. curfew on the ward—she'd completely lost track of time.

"Also time to nurse John again," Lacy said, adjusting her bra, which she bulged out of since her milk had come in.

The sisters stood up and shared a group hug.

"This was really fun," Eva said.

Brynne nodded, having to admit Eva was right, letting contentment fill her, having shared her first special moment with her sisters. Well, a more *normal* special moment, compared with yesterday's delivery of Lacy's baby in the bookstore.

After they escorted Lacy to her room, where a wailing baby waited for her, they said quick goodbyes, including kisses on the cheek, which, also surprisingly, seemed completely normal. Wow, think of all the years she'd missed out on. An ache started in her chest. This was so confusing.

"See you and Paul tomorrow for dinner," Lacy said, no question in the statement. Brynne and Paul, whether engaged or not, were expected, and that was that. No point in protesting. These women were her family. The thought made her smile even as her eyes acted up again, going all misty.

After, Eva and Brynne walked together to their cars.

"Joe's probably wondering where I've been, too,"

she said before stopping by her flashy rental sedan. "But he'll understand. It's not every day a girl meets her triplet." They hugged again."

Buying a dress may have been a failed revenge experiment and nothing more than a fun exercise in shopping online with her sisters, but telling Paul she really did want to marry him was a huge step she still wasn't ready to take. Not without a long, no holds barred talk, where each knew exactly where the other stood. And she definitely wasn't eloping in Vegas just because her newfound sisters were heading that way. Still… "It was fun shopping with you two."

"I know. Plus you got a gorgeous dress."

"For any occasion, right?"

"Right. Now go tell him."

Paul swung open the door to his comfy condo, having let Brynne in through the locked building entrance only seconds before. Looking more relaxed than he'd seen her lately, except for after he'd ravished her at her command last night, she kind of smiled.

"Did you do it?"

"What?" She refused to make it easy for him.

He gave a "you know exactly" stare.

"Buy yourself something?"

"Yes, we did."

"We?"

"Eva and Lacy helped me shop."

"That was probably fun."

"Surprisingly, the whole hanging out with un-known sisters thing was fun."

"Cool."

"There really is some weird connection there."

"You'll have to tell me all about it. But hey, did the therapy shopping work?"

"As in, do I feel better now?"

He made an exaggerated nod.

"Yes. Thank you."

"Cool."

Only then did he kiss her hello, long and slow, as his hands wandered over her neck and back. She felt great and was all present and accounted for, just the way he loved her.

"So we're on for tomorrow night, right? Their house for dinner?"

"I can't *not* go."

"Great." Paul held Brynne at arm's length, study-ing her, uneasy over how uptight she'd just turned. He'd given her six months of breathing room, and all it did was make her more undecided. His now or never approach had backfired. He wasn't sure what else to do. His stomach felt a little sick over the possibility of losing her.

"Come in. Make yourself comfortable." He'd play the perfect host.

"Did you have a chance to get those boxes for me?" She got right down to this business visit. That was okay, because it still gave him a chance to be with her.

"Absolutely." He took her hand and guided her into the main room of his condo. "Would you like a glass of wine?" Thanks to the open-concept design of the condo, the kitchen was a stone's throw from the couch.

"To help sweeten the task? Yes, please!" It was the first sign of enthusiasm he'd seen today.

"Be right back. I'll help, too, once you tell me what we're looking for."

She sat on the edge of the sofa and removed the lid from one of the three cardboard boxes. "Anything like a letter or holiday card saved by Mom from an Allison Roberts."

"Sounds easy enough," he said, removing the cork from a previously opened cabernet sauvignon, sniffing the smooth scent, then pouring two glasses of deep red liquid. "What do we do if we find one?" He carried the wine to Brynne, handed hers off, then taking a sip of his before putting it on a coaster.

"I'm hoping there'll be an address or phone number we can contact her by. The only thing Rory told us was Mom moved here from some place in Santa Barbara."

"That's a fairly big city, and Allison Roberts is a common name. If we don't get a link here, we could still try looking her up in the yellow pages."

"Do they still exist?"

"Online they do. Want me to give it a try now?"

She shrugged as she dug through the first box for anything looking like a stack of letters or holiday cards. Even though he always wondered why people kept such things, he hoped she'd find something to help answer her questions about her birth. Especially since discovering she was a triplet.

"Let's start here, see what we get," she said.

For fun, he checked Santa Barbara yellow pages and found at least fifty Allison Robertses there. After satisfying his curiosity, he happily dug through the second box, fingers crossed they'd come up with something, anything to solve the riddle.

By the end of the first glass of wine, they'd gone through two of the boxes.

"Can I get a refill?" Brynne held up her glass.

"Who am I to argue," he said, heading for the kitchen mumbling the second part. "since I always lose."

"It's been a long night," she said. "Can you just give me a refill without the grief, please."

So he did what he was told.

The third box produced nothing of interest, and Brynne downed the last sips of wine in an irritated way.

It probably wasn't a good time to bring it up, but Paul felt responsible. "You know I can't let you drive home after two glasses of wine."

"Oh, really."

He was a grown man. He could take her snotty

attitude. "Think what you like, but I'm just looking out for you." Yeah, from that skeptical look, she wasn't buying it.

A second later a bolt of lightning lit up the window, drawing their full attention. And a few seconds after that, a loud clap of thunder off in the distance managed to rattle the same window. Soon, loud plops of rain tapped on the roof.

Brynne looked at him incredulously. "Did you text Mother Nature, to keep me here for the night?" By the tipsy absurdity of her comment, she indeed had no business driving home.

"Is that how you feel? That I'm manipulative and I'm making you marry me?"

"I broke off the engagement, and somehow, I still bought a wedding dress tonight."

"Hold on. I didn't tell you to buy a wedding dress, I just suggested you buy yourself something to cheer you up."

"As if that's all I needed."

"And you're obviously mad at me."

"I'm mad at you, at Mom. I'm mad at everyone!

"Why did she have to insist on going to the farmers market and set up her traveling bookstore that weekend? She'd just gotten over a nasty intestinal bug, too, but refused to miss the event. She put herself in the thick of things and walked away with that crazy opportunistic virus, because it was only a few days later when she collapsed at the store.

"Why'd you have to do that, Mom!" Brynne

looked toward the sky as if seeing her mother's face there. "You were always so headstrong and frustratingly independent, and you blew it! This time you died because of it.

"You were supposed to give me away at my wedding. You let me down." She lowered her head and sobbed more. And he held her until she calmed down again.

After what seemed like a very long time, Paul needed to say his thoughts. "Brynne, I swear I'm not trying to fix anything. I'm just going to mention something about life. Is that okay? It's just a personal observation." He held his breath and hoped she'd take it the right way.

Without looking at him, she nodded.

"Getting stuck in anger holds us back. It keeps us angry and resentful, and we risk losing sight of what's important. I'm not telling you to move on or anything, not until you're ready anyway, I'm just mentioning it."

"Why do you have to be so damn nice?" Again, the wine talking, because she couldn't even keep her story straight. Which was it, mad or glad?

If he had to be accused of something, at least nice wasn't so bad. "Because I love you?"

"See, that's what makes me furious. You act like you do things because I need them and I don't know what's good for me."

"That's not the way I see it, or why I do it."

"That's how it feels." Thunder cracked again. The rain pelted harder on the roof.

"I'm sorry."

Her angry eyes studied him, but something had changed behind them. "I just want to figure out what happened with my mom and sisters, and you want to reschedule our wedding."

He bit back his first response—that women usually loved to multitask—because he didn't want her to throw a shoe at him. "And if there is any way I can help you find some answers, I'll do it."

"As long as I marry you?"

He vehemently shook his head. "No. No strings. You want to skip the wedding, I'll understand." The thought made his stomach twist. "For now." If he had to sacrifice marrying her right away to win back her trust, he would. "But you need to talk to me, tell me what's changed, and I don't mean since your sisters showed up. Before."

By her suddenly determined gaze, he realized she'd taken his bait.

"You're completely goal oriented. And we're behind schedule, according to you." She took a step, then paced around the couch as she spoke. "Become an associate professor, check. Get engaged, check. Get tenure, check." She wrote imaginary checks in the air as lightning lit up the room. "Get married. Buy house. Have baby number one. Check, check, check." A clap of thunder emphasized her checks.

"Is that how you see it?"

Another long stare trained at him, his question answered without a word. The earlier queasiness returned, as it sunk into him how he'd come off to her.

"Okay, so I do have a goal of marrying you, because we were supposed to be married in March!" He couldn't help the frustration.

"See, that's what I'm talking about. We missed our scheduled…" She scrunched her face, thinking. "What's the word, nuptials?" Obviously under the effect of two glasses of wine, the term amused her. Was it fair to fight now?

"As much as you feel I'm being unreasonable, can you at least try to see my side of things?" Unlike her, he stood in place, wide stance, arms open, palms up. "We were on track, you loved me, your mother loved me, hell, even Rory loves me. Then overnight everything changed, and I completely understood why. But it's six months now and it keeps changing."

She'd stopped pacing, stood arms akimbo, and to her credit after two glasses of wine, listening.

"I keep losing more and more of you. Instead of getting closer to our life together, we're moving farther away." He seriously hoped the softening in her stare meant she understood.

"A lot is going on in my life, I can't ignore any of it. And now, I have to deal with this before I can move on."

"Again, I understand that, but you still haven't told me what is really holding you back."

He waited hopefully, but her jaw clamped tight.

"Look," he said, stepping toward her, feeling bad for putting her through this when her life had just been turned on its head. Again! But he needed her to know his biggest fear. "While you're digging into your past, I'm just asking you not to forget about your future. Hopefully our future."

She stood still as her eyes closed, then needing to hold the back of the couch to keep steady. At first he thought she might cry, but she quickly shifted her mood.

"And disappoint my 'sisters'?" She put air quotes around "sisters." Her sarcasm proved she was all mixed up about them turning up in her life at this sticky interlude, too. Would there ever be a perfect time for them to get married? She stared at her toes as he moved closer—only then did he realize she'd kicked off her shoes, standing there, toes digging into his fluffy throw rug.

"What do you mean, disappoint your sisters?"

"They talked me into buying a wedding dress tonight!"

Hope shot through him like another bolt of lightning, even as her attitude sunk in.

"I did not put them up to that."

"I know."

He let her be for a good minute as he finished his wine. Then he shrugged. "At the risk of ticking you off more, for the record, now that I've had two drinks, I can't drive you home, either."

She walked around the couch and kicked the nearest box, the third box, with bare toes and hopped around for a few seconds as a result. "This is so frustrating!"

He completely understood that "this" meant "everything!" Plus, they'd come up with nothing, and Brynne looked both frustrated and disappointed after a long, exaggerated sigh.

He needed clarification, though, because he'd meant to be charming, in a teasing kind of way, and she was kicking boxes. "What's so frustrating?"

"That we can't figure out what the hell my mom was up to! And we don't have anyone to ask, because Rory is a waste of time in the answer department." She lifted her empty glass toward him. "Can you pour me another?" So maybe she'd come to terms with not going home tonight.

He obliged her wish quickly, only wanting to please. And to keep her there.

"So frustrating!" She practically growled from the other room. He heard another foot thud on the box and settled on half a refill, adding water.

She'd painted a picture of who he was, and it had hurt. He could understand how that might come off as unappealing. He'd change, some way, somehow, for her. No pressure. But in his gut, he still wondered what really held her back. Well, besides every little gripe she'd gladly poured out about him. There was no doubt about one thing, though. He knew how they were completely compatible, and he wasn't going to let her forget it.

He hurried back into the living room, gave her the half glass of wine, helped her sit down, then took her free hand in his. When he had her full attention, he lightly kissed each knuckle before connecting with her tortured blue eyes. Probably against her will, but she still liked him doing that. A lot. "I've got an app for that," he whispered.

"For finding unnamed relatives or friends?" She'd gone from tipsy box kicking to acerbic in record time. She also took a generous drink from the glass in her free hand. Fortunately she didn't notice it was mostly water.

"An app for how to fix your frustration."

One of her perfectly shaped brows lifted in interest, so he kissed his way up the fine skin of her arm to the inside of her elbow. There, he planted a whisper of a kiss, making her flesh break out in chill bumps. He enjoyed watching every single one.

Her head tilted, and from beneath her mascara, she gave him a perceptive gaze. At this rate, he predicted he'd soon be kissing his way to the back of her knees, and from there…?

"A temporary fix," she stated, taking some of the air from his sails. He continued to kiss the inside of her elbow while rain pelted the windows until the next sigh escaping her lips sounded in an entirely different class.

After her blissful moan, signaling his kisses were

on the perfect path, he still needed to make sure. "Would you like to join me in bed?"

She swallowed and watched him closely for several moments. "Sleep with my ex-fiancé? How daring."

"Then I dare you."

Chapter Seven

Monday night at the huge rental, Eva proved to be the perfect hostess. Her idea of casual was evidently chic. Wearing off-white wide-leg cotton gauze lounge pants, a light brown loose crocheted sweater with one centrally located button over a white tank top, and a larger-than-life seashell assortment necklace, she looked ready for a photo shoot rather than a takeout dinner with her sisters. Especially since her hair was in an updo.

Brynne, with her usual braid, was impressed, though worried about being a little dowdy in her jeans and three-quarter-sleeved cotton top combo, even though she'd left home feeling daring—a feeling that had started last night at Paul's condo—wearing her favorite shade of deep purple to complement her hair. At least she'd bypassed her usual sneakers for a sporty pair of Skechers, admittedly only doing so to dress up a bit. Wow, had she undershot the mark.

Obviously caring less about what Brynne had worn, Eva was thrilled to see her. She further proved it by rushing in for a hug and a peck on the cheek. Brynne usually shied away from big shows of affection, something she only let her mom do, and less often, Rory, and she inwardly tensed while pretending to welcome it. Sisters or not, Eva was still a stranger.

"Am I being pushy?" Eva asked close to her ear.

"No," Brynne fibbed.

Joe—with Noah, the black-haired toddler, slung over the side of his jeans-clad hip, squiggling and acting like he wasn't really enjoying every part of the awkward position—glad-handed Paul and obviously made him feel at home. But Paul felt at home anywhere, for which Brynne envied him.

Zack casually looked on, waiting his turn to say hi, with a longneck in hand. "Hey, can I get you one?" he said after a double tap to Paul's deltoid in greeting.

Paul nodded his thanks—"Sounds good"—and as usual, he fit right in. Big family versus loner mom—yeah, the dynamic made a difference. Not that a big family automatically created an extrovert and vice versa, but it certainly had in Paul and

Brynne's case, and she'd noticed the difference right from the start.

Lacy, just coming off a nursing session with John, looked especially excited about the food. Wearing a colorful patterned tunic and black leggings, she looked right at home as she grabbed a chicken leg and chomped on it. "Excuse me, but I'm starving. Like, all the time." After a quick chew and swallow, she was ready to go again. "It's so good to be out of the hospital. No offense, Brynne, but the food was awful."

Now this was a topic she was an expert on.

"It's supposed to be." Paul spoke up, beating her to the punch. "It's all part of the subversive plan to get people to want to go home quicker."

Paul's good mood had everything to do with the surroundings. He was in his element—the man loved being around people. Though the fact they'd been hitting the sheets significantly more than usual probably had a lot deal to do with his relaxed and perpetual smile. Was that a normal consequence of breaking an engagement? Miffed he'd stolen her thunder on hospital-cafeteria knowledge, she forced a grin while grinding her molars.

Eva had found the best caterers in town in less than twenty-four hours, evidently another effortless knack of the wealthy, and the spread of food laid out on the extralong dining table looked delicious. Like Lacy, Brynne was ready to grab a sample.

In the background, the state-of-the-art kitchen

was big enough to comfortably accommodate all the adults, plus little Emma, Noah and both the babies, thanks to the supersize island. Still, Eva had chosen the dining table, making Brynne feel like the guest of honor.

Emma knelt on the floor across the room and watched Estrella as she sat on a blanket and rattled and shook everything she could get her pudgy little fingers on, though only after tasting it first. The rental must have come stocked with family items. Once again, Brynne was impressed that a house in her hometown was perfectly suited for a *Modern Home and Design* magazine cover.

"Let's do this buffet-style and then we can all go out on the deck to eat," Eva said. "You won't believe the view." She handed Brynne the first plate, continuing to make her feel special. Then it quickly occurred that she probably was, being the newest twin and all. They'd both been through it before, but Brynne hadn't.

She stepped outside, and the mountainous views from her city were anything but a surprise, never taken for granted and always appreciated. Still, they looked extra beautiful tonight. Was it the company?

"Ooh, Paul," Lacy said, once everyone was outside enjoying their meal. "You should see the *sexy* dress we picked out for Brynne last night."

"I can't wait," Paul said a tad overenthusiastic.

He carried on, making easy conversation. He'd been trained well by his clan. And she'd been raised by a private woman who enjoyed the sound of silence and reading books. This was all foreign territory, and that kept her from completely relaxing. They were all still practically strangers, she reminded herself again and again. Though, one odd thing—she'd never gotten this close to strangers so quickly. Lacy and Eva were the pretend sisters she used to have imaginary conversations with. The thought sent a chill over her spine.

Still, she made a mental note to ask them later if they'd ever done that, too.

Paul sat beside her, his plate already half-empty. "Hey, guys," Paul said, voice raised, as natural as could be, having only met everyone in the last two days. "My dad is making lasagna in your honor, so I just wanted to remind you that dinner will be at the Capriati house tomorrow."

His announcement was met with cheers—"Yay, Italian food"—and quickly the men hashed out the time.

Tension ran a lap around Brynne's entire body at the thought of all this plus Paul's family in one house. Would it be more than she could handle?

She glanced around at everyone, all in good spirits. She, on the other hand, fighting her discomfort. This unknown family had found her, and if she was honest, it was exciting. Why not enjoy them?

Lacy and Eva migrated toward Brynne, and as things settled down while everyone ate, they spoke quietly and happily, making small talk, working hard on their crash course task of getting to know each other.

"What was your favorite movie when you were a kid?" Lacy asked, chomping on a dinner roll.

Her out-of-the-blue question sent Brynne on a quick trip down memory lane. "Hands down, *The Princess Bride*," she said. Her mom had been choosy over what she'd let Brynne watch, and this one had passed the test.

"Loved that one," Lacy replied, enthusiasm as obvious as her hand gestures. "I think Westley was my first crush."

"Mine was the kid from *The Neverending Story*," Eva said. "Atreyu was so hot."

Silly as it was, this harmless conversation felt safer than others, and Brynne easily shared. "I loved that one, too," she chimed in as memories of being a lonely little girl watching rental fantasy movies on Friday nights rushed back. Bittersweet memories that, if she were honest, might've been nicer if she'd had friends—or sisters—to share them with. Even as an adult, her "friends" tended to be people she worked with.

"Have you seen him as an adult?" Lacy said. "The looks didn't transfer."

The comment caught Brynne off guard and made her laugh. Lacy was a character, and, ready or not, she was growing on Brynne.

To back up her story, Lacy googled it and shared the results. They all agreed and laughed—and wow, how natural did it feel to be having this immature discussion? Then it occurred to her that the many other conversations they'd missed could never be made up, but right here, right now, they just went for it.

Even though it was against her nature, Brynne had come prepared, thanks in no small part to rummaging through those old boxes.

"Oh hey, I brought pictures," Brynne said, leading them inside then grabbing from her purse the old-school photo prints she'd snagged last night. At least she had them to offer.

Eva and Lacy were eager to finally see their birth mother, as Brynne shared the lot of them. Jessica Taylor had been of average height, with thick light brown, full-bodied hair that she'd preferred to keep short. She was naturally on the scrawny side, her eyes were hazel green, her smile stellar.

"Wow. So that's our mom," Lacy said while they all stopped to think about it.

With near reverence, she passed the pictures to Eva, and Brynne looked on, wondering how it must feel for them. She'd had something they'd both missed out on. Lacy had her dad—*their* dad—and though Brynne wasn't sure how she felt about it, there was still curiosity about what he must have been like. Eva didn't have either birth parent in her life, but she'd been raised never wanting for a material thing. Brynne wondered what she would've given to know them. As she considered these things, a small part of her bulletproof glass barrier started to come down.

"I think we all have her nose," Eva said, as matter-of-fact as could be.

"We definitely do." Brynne had known that her entire life—for them it was a revelation. Again, what must they be thinking? Feeling?

"She has really kind eyes," Lacy commented, smiling as hers went misty.

"Mom was patient and gentle, but she had a temper."

"Like throw-things-across-the-room temper?" Lacy's immediate curiosity put a stop to her near tears.

"More like the look of death, and I never wanted to cross her to find out if she was bluffing or not."

They laughed, and the sound touched Brynne's heart, being the expert on Jessica Taylor, professional surrogate. The thought bumped into Brynne and momentarily knocked her off balance. All the things she'd never known about Mom.

"Wow, the mystery woman, our birth mother," Eva said, staring at one picture in particular and growing serious just as quickly as they'd laughed the moment before. For the next few seconds, she sat quietly inspecting each picture, as though hunting for a clue on why Jessica had separated her daughters.

"The woman from the bookstore seems to be in

a lot of these pictures," Lacy said, scrunching up her eyes to look closer.

"Rory. Yes, she was Mom's best friend, like a second mom to me. We were kind of like this little misfit family. They looked out for each other," Brynne said, not even blinking at how involved Rory had been in her life since the day she'd moved here. Because that was just the way it always had been. "Now, please, please, please, show me some pictures of our dad."

Lacy was happy to oblige, but unlike Brynne, she had her photos on the cell phone. She retrieved it and quickly brought up the albums section. "He's the source of our hair, obviously."

Brynne marveled at seeing a man with a natural smile and more than a dusting of freckles on his face. "And the blue eyes," she said, taking her first look at the man who'd come up with the idea of hiring a surrogate. Her birth father. He had unruly bright red hair that topped his head in a lopsided fashion. Maybe time for a haircut? She zoomed in on his eyes. Yes, they were the same pale blue color. In each picture, he had that great broad smile and a strong jaw. Brynne's and her sister's jaws were petite and a little pointy, more like their mom's. Her first impression was that she liked him. Then she quickly wondered how different her life would've been if he'd been able to support triplets.

A moot thought that caused a hard feeling to hit the pit of her stomach.

John Winters looked kind, but scrappy, too, like a typical working man. A man who couldn't afford raising three children. Who had carried one hell of a secret to his grave. She needed to cut him some slack, since her mother had done the same, but man, it was hard. If she let herself be angry at him, she'd have to be mad at her mother, too, which she'd discovered last night, she was. Her thoughts must have seeped out to Eva and Lacy, since they all went quiet and looked a little sad.

"We can't change history, right?" Eva stated the fact.

"Nope," Brynne agreed.

"But we can start our history today," Lacy said, taking Brynne's hand. "Even though you live in Utah, we've got to promise to spend the big holidays together. Come to California for Christmas?"

Unsure of jumping right in feetfirst, Brynne shied away from the invitation. "Or you guys could come here to ski."

"Definitely," Eva said. "And summers, we can all meet somewhere and rent a huge house like this so we can stay together and vacation."

Was that what she wanted? It sounded so normal. Brynne knew that soon her sisters would be back in their homes, far away, and all these little plans could very well never happen. The question was, how did she feel about that? It was safer to go back to how things were before they'd met, which held a lot of appeal. But now that she'd found Lacy and Eva, could they ever be the same? What was wrong with keeping in touch?

"And our first family trip together could be a destination wedding in Las Vegas, woo hoo!" Lacy said, pretending to toss confetti. That put the brakes on the happy moment.

"Well, I wouldn't go that far."

"Sorry. I have a tendency to go overboard."

"I'll forgive you this time."

Things got quiet for the next few seconds, and worrying she'd been the cause, Brynne brought up another subject. "Did you guys used to feel like something was missing? It's hard to explain, but like, when I was little, I used to talk to my pretend sisters. Not just one, but two. I swear."

Instead of finding disbelief in their eyes, she found recognition and agreement, and she didn't need to explain a single thing more. They both solemnly nodded.

"I always wanted a sister," Lacy said. "I longed for someone to share my deepest secrets with."

"And I always felt this huge chunk of me was missing. I was a super-lonely child," Eva said, provoking a group hug.

For Brynne, sitting with these women in the sunken living room, off in the corner where a sofa and chair were arranged specifically for such private conversations, she'd never felt so much a part of something in her life. What a revelation. It helped her relax and, inwardly smiling, she let the sensations of completely belonging to something bigger than herself trickle over her. Being honest, it felt great. Why fight it? She'd stumbled upon her sisters from birth. It really was far bleeping out!

A couple hours later, after the men considerately took care of the kids and cleanup, allowing Lacy, Eva and Brynne their special time together, Paul reluctantly approached. "I hate to be the one to break this up, but I've got to prepare for tomorrow."

Tuesdays were his busiest, with extra classes and university admin meetings. Brynne understood, and neither Eva nor Lacy seemed to hold a grudge.

"I'd be glad to drive you home," Zack said, "if you'd like to stick around?"

"Thanks so much," Brynne said, "but since I'm taking the week off, I've just made plans to meet my sisters for lunch tomorrow." Finally saying it aloud felt weird and wonderful at once. A tiny shiver hit her neck.

What if she gave in to Paul's idea and just went for it, got married? Though the brakes were letting up with her sisters, they still felt intact on rushing a wedding. Though after last night's shouting session, she felt he understood better why, and he'd nearly broken her heart with how he worried about losing sight of the future.

On the way out, Lacy clapped her hands. "I can't wait for lunch!"

Eva gave Brynne a droll expression. "Pardon our

sister but she gets easily carried away especially where food is concerned."

As easy as bubbling water, they chuckled together, and Brynne began to feel a part of something much bigger than herself. So this was what family was like. She and her mother had been tight, for sure, but being honest, it had felt more like a team of two, well, three counting Rory, than this. Family.

For the first time since meeting Paul, she nearly grasped what he'd been trying to tell her. A big family could be a good thing. If she could just wrap her brain around motherhood.

"I'm excited, too," Brynne said, surprising herself and bringing on another group hug.

Their extended goodbyes were packed with quick add-ons like, "I still don't know your favorite color."

"Did you hate tuna salad when you were a kid, too?"

"When did you start wearing a bra?" as though fighting for more time and information on the spot, and finally, "Write all the questions down and we'll talk about them tomorrow," suggested by Eva. Finally, Brynne and Paul left.

Unlike her usual self, Brynne chatted away the whole ride home to her apartment. "It's like we're picking up where we left off, except we never had a before, before. But it doesn't matter, because it seems we already know each other." She went quiet for a few seconds. "Is that possible?"

"Apparently," Paul said. When he looked at her, she beamed with enthusiasm.

"I understand you probably have a lot going on in your head, and I'm happy for you. But just in case you're wondering how you'll ever be able to go to sleep after all this, well, I'm just throwing it out there—"

"Yes," she interrupted, answering his question before he'd been able to get it out. "Let's go to your house."

Wow, talk about having the honeymoon before the wedding. Which was on hold. Indefinitely?

Brynne hadn't met her sisters until two days ago, and they were the injection of excitement he hadn't seen in her since her mother died.

So, was he taking advantage of her? Of course not—all he had to do was look at her, as positive as could be with her yes before he'd asked her to sleep over. She needed him, and he needed her, which, as history had proved with them, equaled mutual satisfaction.

Tuesday night, in Paul's family home, was best described as controlled chaos. The cozy house where he'd grown up was packed with three red-heads and their significant others, including their four kids, Mom, Dad and Nona. Feeling cramped, he wondered how the four siblings had managed to make it through high school without permanent elbow marks embedded in their torsos. Still, he smiled, because he loved the noise and having to turn sideways to make it through the kitchen door because of the constant activity.

His maternal grandma, all four feet eleven of her, at eighty-two, having taken up permanent residence with his folks, could still light up a room. Which she was currently doing with the triplets, no doubt embarrassing him with stories about his childhood through Nona's memory. That could mean a blending of tales about his two brothers and sister, with maybe a touch of him thrown in.

She'd obviously gotten her monthly perm, her still mostly black hair cropped short and now curled tight enough not to require combing for days. Somewhere over the years her torso and waist had sunk straight to her hips, making her even shorter and inclining her toward loose blouses. Today's top was bright yellow, over navy-blue polyester stretch-waist pants. She'd given up on zippers and heels years ago and now spent most of her time looking up people's noses when in conversation. But she seemed thrilled to be talking to Brynne, Lacy and Eva. Her sweet crinkly eyes were shining as they spoke.

Dad, still almost as tall as Paul, though hunched some for sure, supervised the best-smelling-and-tasting lasagna in town. At least that's what Dad had told him his entire life. His hair was mostly silver now, and Paul liked how it made him look distinguished. The guy deserved unending kudos for spending his entire working life as a middle school teacher, which was also probably why he'd gone prematurely gray.

Mom scuttled around the small kitchen taking care of everything else, which, in this Italian home meant multiple side dishes and bread. Of course, bread. Because life would end otherwise.

Zack's daughter, Emma, had taken up residence nearby, watching in awe all the cooking and preparing as though it was the best reality show on earth. From what he'd learned from Lacy, Emma had dreams of becoming a chef one day.

"Ma, let Emma stir the sauce," Paul suggested, and once Eleanora Capriati caught on, she gave undivided attention to the young one's culinary experience, even offering her Nona's stool to stand on.

Mom still kept her hair blond and big. *Bouffant* was the word she'd always used. Like in the '70s, but tastefully clipped to just below her earlobes, if *tasteful* and *'70s* wasn't already a contradiction.

Zack and Joe had been treated like kings by Mom and Nona since they'd arrived—which probably had something to do with them once again being in charge of childcare—and they were currently lounging in the two comfortable recliners attached to each end of the sectional sofa, nibbling on homemade bruschetta, which Paul knew for a fact was the best in the world. Again, because Nona told him so.

Paul had made a point to carve out some intentional time with Brynne tonight. Nonsexual time, which they'd had surprisingly a lot of for not currently being engaged. She'd promised to make time for him, too, though admittedly he'd asked during a crucial moment late last night, and her first answer had been "Don't stop!" Before arriving tonight, he'd reminded her of her agreement, and that he understood he'd have to wait until after the meal to get her alone.

From the expression on her face, he sensed she expected him to ask her to marry him again. Well, she'd be surprised, since that wasn't part of his plan.

Nona banged the lid of a pot with a metal serving spoon. "Dinner is served," she said, the hint of her Sicilian upbringing still evident. *"Mangiare!"*

"Seems like we just finished our lunch together," Lacy said to Brynne and Eva as they headed to the table.

"Being a nurse, I'm not used to three-hour lunches," Brynne said easily, as though she was starting to get the hang of being a triplet. "But I could!"

"Aren't you an independent small-business woman these days?" Eva said, putting her freshly manicured hand on Brynne's shoulder. She didn't even seem to flinch. A great sign. "You can make your own hours for lunch, right?"

Brynne chuckled. "I see you're assuming I'm a highly successful business owner."

"I'm sure you will be," Eva said, a confident glint in her eyes.

Paul hoped that confidence would rub off on Brynne. She'd been doing a great job under the circumstances of stepping into a business she knew nothing about. Fortunately, it was an established bookstore, but it had fallen into a common rut— resting on the regular customers instead of reaching out to new ones. There was work to be done, and Paul was certain Brynne would rise to the challenge. In his mind, there was nothing she couldn't do. That was, except marry him, apparently.

Somehow, though cramped and with little room to spare, the crowd all managed to make it around the heirloom dining table, with all three center leaves in place. The same old oak table around which he'd grown up celebrating every major— and several minor—holidays every year of his life.

And as Dad had promised, the lasagna was world-class. From the blissful looks on the guests' faces, they agreed.

Paul sat next to Brynne, who seemed more relaxed than usual when at his house, maybe because there were three of her tonight, and she didn't feel under the microscope as she usually did. He understood it had to be tough coming from a single-mom and child home, having to transition to his family, especially when all four of the siblings were also in attendance. But as he looked around the table at his mom, dad and Nona happily sharing their food and entertaining their guests, he wondered, what wasn't to love about the Capriati *famiglia*?

After dinner and cleanup, he planned to make his move on Brynne. Having sensed her being swept away since discovering her sisters and the Pandora's box they opened, he'd made plans for some quiet time together. They needed to talk. Unlike the frantic sex they'd been sharing—since apparently meeting her unknown family sparked and released loads of passionate energy—their usual conversations, from before she'd broken off the engagement, had become a forgotten art.

"Getting used to the chaos yet?" he asked as he edged his way beside her in a corner of the kitchen. Loud talking and laughter filled in the background.

"I'm working on it," she said, overall looking happy while putting dishes in the cupboard, though still a little overwhelmed, too.

"Did you see the look on Mom's face when she saw three of you?" he said, handing her the next batch of plates. He couldn't help the grin, since rarely had he seen his mother, a Realtor and shrewd judge of character, caught off guard by anything or anyone.

"Oh my gosh, that was classic. Wish we'd gotten it on video."

"I think Joe did. Or Zack. One of them."

She turned to take the next batch of saucers while standing on Nona's stool. "You like them, don't you," she said. It wasn't a question about her new family and in-laws.

"I do, they're great, down-to-earth people. Easy to know and be around."

"I thought it was just me—after I quit resisting, anyway. Good to know you feel the same."

"Yeah, good thing, too, because we're going to be seeing a lot of them the rest of our lives."

The phrase slipped out as naturally as the latest time he'd told her he loved her. He knew they belonged together, but he caught the glint of shock in her eyes when he'd so casually said, "the rest of our lives." In her mind they were no longer engaged, and here he was pushing like nothing had changed.

She'd also finished her task of putting away the dishes, so he took her hand and led her into the hallway, away from the rest.

"I understand it's a big deal having your world turned on its ear over a single week, but we'll make it work. You'll see—everything will be fine."

"You're leaving something important out."

He knew, of course he did, but he chose to ignore their breakup. "No. I'm choosing to forget the past and look to the future."

"You're not being fair. I need some say in this."

"I want nothing more."

"Than for me to say yes, but I'm still not there yet. Especially now."

"I get it, but they'll all be going home, and I'll be here. I want—"

"I know what you want."

He nodded, choosing not to press the point that he knew beyond all else. They belonged together.

From her sudden silence, the last thing he felt was that everything would eventually be okay. Good thing he had his knock-it-out-of-the-park surprise. One he'd sworn his mother to silence on.

"Uh, getting back to tomorrow. You and I need some alone time, outdoors, where we won't get distracted by the bedroom and can't get in trouble." It occurred that the overabundance of stress in her life might push her to new heights. Picnic-blanket sex hadn't occurred to him, but who knew what she might talk him into?

"What are you smiling about?"

"Oh, nothing," he said. "But I have the perfect spot in mind, and we'll have a picnic. Just you and me. Okay?"

And as any woman whose life had been taken over by surprise circumstances with long-lost relatives and forced weddings would do, she robotically nodded her head.

Since she'd read off her list of complaints last night, he understood her resistance more, and vowed to change. For her.

He smiled and bussed her cheek. Man, he loved her. He also had a bombshell surprise to lay on her that might possibly overpower the shock of discovering she was a triplet. Which made him have second thoughts. In his defense, he'd planned it long before the breakup. But damn, she'd mocked his checking off boxes last night. Maybe he had more thinking to do tonight.

Chapter Eight

His mom had met Paul's specifications to a T with the property she'd found. Three bedrooms plus a den, huge family room, updated kitchen and bathrooms. An older home but move-in ready, waiting for Brynne and Paul to make it theirs. It was away from downtown Cedars in the City, yet within a fifteen- to twenty-minute drive of just about anywhere they'd need to go.

He'd been anxious to start his life with Brynne in this house and could see them living there for years to come.

But that was before she'd called him out for being too goal oriented. All during the night he'd had second thoughts about this supposedly big reveal, one where she'd clap her hands together and declare,

"How soon can we get married?" Man, was he out of touch with the woman he loved, and it was about time he did something about that.

She stood waiting outside the bookshop in jeans and a bright green top, her hair being the first thing he spotted about her, as usual in the long braid. The sight of Brynne always made him smile, even now, during her reluctant-fiancée phase.

He still couldn't figure out why she'd been as eager to get married as him last spring and now had changed. He'd been the same goal-oriented guy, why didn't it bother her then?

When this house first came on the market, he'd hoped it would help her see their future. But with the appearance of her sisters—who knew, she might want to move to California. Since breaking up on Saturday, every part of his future seemed up in the air, and he wanted desperately to do something about that. Well, here goes.

"You look chipper," he said after he'd pulled to the curb and she climbed in.

"I had a surprisingly good night's sleep."

"Wish I could've been there."

She gave him a droll stare. "You know as well as I, then we'd both be bleary eyed."

He reached over and squeezed her knee. "But for a great reason."

Her smiles came easy, which was encouraging. He could only hope after the big surprise later, she'd smile more.

After a twenty-minute drive outside town, at the huge Eureka Park, he pulled in the middle school lot and they walked to a grove of trees. He threw down the old and holey blanket from the trunk of his car and they sat.

"Hope you don't mind Italian subs?" He fished two paper-wrapped sandwiches from the large brown bag in the small cooler he'd brought along. "And canned flavored tea?"

"Green?"

"Of course." He knew his fiancée's tastes.

"Sounds good. It's a beautiful day."

"Perfect weather."

"We need to tell Lacy and Eva about Eureka Park. The kids would have a ball here."

"Great idea," he said, taking a guy-size first bite, the deli meats and provolone cheese hitting his mouth in a burst thanks to the added peppers. For a few moments they ate peacefully, both enjoying the brisk, fresh air and sunshine.

"You seem to be getting along great with your sisters," he said between bites.

"I wasn't sure at first, but it seems that way. They're both so nice, and in different ways. Lacy makes me laugh and Eva makes me want to develop a better fashion sense, and I like them equally." She stole one of his barbecue chips and crunched.

He took one of her baked potato chips, did the same. "It's got to be crazy finding out you're a triplet."

"Beyond words." She took a long drink from her peach-infused green tea. "I feel like I should be even more mad at Mom, but I can't bring myself to feel that way."

"She was doing what she felt was best at the time, most likely." Finances had to be the main reason, he guessed, but had desperation been the true motivation? Like Brynne, Paul wished Jessica was here to answer their endless questions.

"With no idea of the repercussions." She stopped eating, giving him a long, thoughtful gaze. "Is this what you wanted to talk about?"

"Not completely. I've been thinking about what you told me the other night, about being too goal oriented. The check, check, checking, and well, I'm gonna work on it."

"That's great," Brynne said, surprisingly impressed. "Thank you."

He nodded. "But I'd made one little plan a while before you made your point."

"I'm not surprised. Which was?"

"I'm not sure now is a good time, but when you're done eating, I'd like to take a walk." He pointed out the trail scattered with leaves and small puddles from the other night's storm that circled the entire Eureka Park area.

"Okay." She took another bite of her sandwich. "Did you know we all had breakfast together this morning?"

"Really?" She'd gone far beyond dipping her toes

in the water to wading farther and deeper into her new family. Good for her. And maybe good for him, since Lacy and Eva might have some influence over her being stuck. "Might be harder than you think when they go home."

"You have a point. But I can't not get to know them and we've promised to stay in touch. Like a regular family."

He wished she'd use the same reasoning about marrying him. *She can't not.* "What changed your mind?"

She shook her head as her shoulders lifted on a deep breath, sandwich held suspended midway to her mouth. "Besides the fact we have the same DNA, they're just good people."

He was a good person, too—she knew that. At risk of making everything about him, which was the opposite of what he intended to do, he opted to keep the thought to himself. "Could you imagine if your mom knew this might happen?"

"I've been thinking about that, and I suspect that's why we lived the way we did. Quiet. Isolated. She never wanted it to happen. And her being practically a recluse shaped our whole lives. I think she must've always been looking over her shoulder."

Now was as good a time as any to broach the topic front and center from his earlier musing. "Do you think being brought up that way is one more reason you feel so resistant to getting married?"

She went inward a moment. "My mom never

needed a man. It wasn't like she was sitting around and waiting for one, but she wasn't looking, either. She went on with her life, learned to be completely independent, and expected me to be the same. Which made her my anchor, and I've felt lost without her."

"You haven't got a dependent bone in your body. Your mother did a fine job raising you."

She shrugged. "I'm glad you see it that way."

"You just stepped right up and took over the bookstore, and…"

"I'd grown up with it, and always loved it. Hell, I've lived above it for the last ten years. But that store was my mother's dream."

She finished her tea and wrapped up the half-eaten sub sandwich. "I don't want to be my mother."

"Understood. So let Rory take over."

"I've been thinking about that, too. But how many more changes can I take at once?"

Point taken.

"Then this probably isn't the greatest time to take that walk, but I'd like you to see something. Because, these days, is there ever a good time?"

From the flash in her eyes, she must've known this was important. He'd promised not to ask her to marry him again, not today anyway, so she didn't have to worry about that, but if he led her to the house that he wanted to put a bid in for, after everything she'd told him the other night, it might be the last time he saw her. Still, because he loved her so much, he felt compelled to take the risk. Because that was what a desperate man did. He reached out for her hand, and she took his. "Let's just take a walk."

He put the blanket in the trunk and trash in the nearest can. After putting the uneaten food back in the small cooler in the car, they headed toward the wide path.

"There aren't many houses in this area," she said casually.

"I know."

"It's pretty. I like it."

"Could you see yourself living out here?"

"With you?" She gave him a long silent stare.

"Okay, I'm pushing things again, I see."

Instead of pushing him away, she didn't let go of his hand, so they kept walking. After half a mile, they approached a lane with a long gravel driveway leading to a two-story house set off from the street. "Want to check it out?"

"The house?"

He nodded. "It's older, but that's what I like about it—has more character."

"Wait, we're looking at a house right now? One you've seen before?"

Another nod, this one sheepish. "Look, that was the old me, the guy who ticks boxes. But I'm fine with just walking today."

"We just happened to be in the neighborhood?"

"Yeah. You could say that." He took her hand and pulled her the other way. "Let's keep walking."

"Well, now that you've piqued my interest, that isn't fair. How long have you been looking for houses?"

"Since before March. But I never saw anything I could visualize us in...until this one."

"When did you find it?"

"The day before you broke off the engagement."

"Oh, man, I really ruined your plans."

"Yeah, so why do you look so pleased about that?"

"It helps drive my point home about you."

"Okay, like I said, I get it. Come on, let's go." He tried to lead her away, but she resisted.

"How'd you find it?"

"Mom found the listing, got me the key. We don't have to look at it."

She dug in, refusing to follow him. "Well, guess what, I'm curious to see the house you see us living in. See if I agree."

"As long as you don't feel..."

"Manipulated?"

He sighed. "Yeah, that."

The house was log cabin–styled, two stories, with a big wraparound porch and wide front steps. With a simple front door, but large windows on either side of it. Paul unlocked and opened the door, allowing Brynne to enter.

Brynne took a step inside, curious. Instead of

being dark and dreary as she usually found log cabin homes, this one was open and bright from added skylights and high windows placed strategically in every wall. Not bad.

"The kitchen's all new. You'll love this island with the sink in it, handy to all the counters." Trained well by his Realtor mother, Paul pointed out the conveniences.

"But I barely cook."

"Lacy can teach both of us." He grinned, and she saw in his eyes the need for her to see the magic he'd found here. She wasn't sure she had. Yet. "We can learn together." He continued the tour.

"And back here is an office, den or guest room, whatever you want to call it, close to a centrally located bathroom for the entire downstairs." He took her hand, pulled her into it. "When your sisters come to visit, it'll be plenty big for them, plus there are three more bedrooms upstairs. Want to see?"

With all the bedrooms, it was clear what he had in mind. A family like his. He'd already forgotten their first bargain, made before their wedding was planned. One at a time.

She followed him upstairs, trying her best to visualize herself living here, not sure she could.

They didn't need a house this size. Couldn't they start small and work their way up, but only if necessary?

"Look at this master bedroom." He dragged her immediately to the long sliding glass doors. "Look at that view! And we've got a private deck." He opened them, and they stepped outside. "Can you see us watching the stars from here?"

She glanced up at the huge blue Utah sky, only wispy clouds in sight along with a pale sliver of moon in the broad daylight. She couldn't deny it was a stunning vista. And there was loads of privacy.

"Check out the bathroom. You can practically sail a boat in that soaking tub." A large shower surrounded entirely by glass was in the far corner. The tub sat in the center of the long bathroom wall. He wasn't lying—the house had a lot to offer. But could she see herself living here?

"It's beautiful. I agree."

"But," he said, on to her unsure tone. "I hear a *but* in there."

How much longer would he put up with her dragging her feet about everything before giving up? It worried her, but she couldn't shake her hesitation, when her feet and heart felt stuck in cement.

"There's that walking path right beyond our property—I mean, the property. And all kinds of trails. Good for cross-country skiing in winter. And look at the fenced-in yard. We could have a dog. You've always wanted a dog."

Man, he was doing the big sell, and it only made her recoil. All the great things about this house, with a little more character than the usual Cedars in the City home, were falling on plugged ears and veiled eyes. He'd been right to worry she'd lost sight of the future.

She had to give him some kind of reaction. "It does seem nice, Paul." More than nice, but she wasn't ready to admit it.

"The thing is, I'm ready to make an offer, put a down payment on it. Just say the word."

"When we're ready to buy a house, I'd want us to find one together."

She saw the disappointment. "I know you expected me to fall in love at first sight, like you did. And I really do like it, but."

"But the timing is off, I get it."

He was being surprisingly understanding. "Was this the first house you looked at?"

"Well, actually, no. I've probably seen dozens over the past six months, but this is the only one I wanted you to see."

"You looked at a dozen homes without me?"

"I knew you weren't in the right frame of mind. And it helped me hold on to my dream for us. Sorry, but I'm being honest here."

"Thank you. It must have been horribly hard for you all this time, keeping these secrets." She'd focused so much on herself, instead of accusing Paul of taking her for granted, she needed to see how much she'd taken him for granted. "It is sort of sweet, in a torqued kind of way."

He was willing to laugh at himself.

"After my sisters leave, I'd be open to looking at more."

"Well, that's a start then."

"That way, we'd both be sure. I need to be sure, see what's out there." It wasn't Paul she was unsure of—it was the life she thought he expected her to live.

"Okay. When you're ready we'll look at more."

Before they left, they checked out both the other bedrooms, each with a unique and lovely view, then went back downstairs.

"As irritating as I've been to you lately," Paul said, "I just want to remind you that your mother loved me. Don't forget that. She was happy we were getting married."

"I know that. Rory loves you, too." It was true. Mom had adored Paul, so did Rory. They'd trusted he'd be a good husband, given Brynne their blessing for the marriage. Then Mom got sick and died. "I know," she said, barely audible.

Paul didn't push her today, not at all like at the Rusty Nail. He'd stopped talking about the house as they headed for home, so they drove in silence. She couldn't ignore the fact he was way ahead of her. He saw them married and living in that house. For the rest of their lives? And she was still stuck on the fine print. Would she be able to work? How many kids? Could she handle a family without her mother's help?

Yes, they'd talked about everything long ago, but

that was before her world had changed, and she'd inherited a bookstore. Now she had no clue how to make it all work.

When he dropped her off at the bookstore, he got out of the car, hugged and kissed her. She knew he had a late-afternoon class on Wednesdays so didn't think it abrupt.

"I'm glad you kind of liked the house," he said just before sliding back behind the wheel.

"It was really nice."

"Well, that's something, at least."

He waved and drove off, and it occurred to her that this was the first time he'd left without saying he loved her.

Brynne entered her store from the front, waving hello to Nate behind the counter and noticing Rory stocking books in the romance section toward the back. "Hey, Ror" was all she said.

Rory turned and smiled, pushed her glasses up the bridge of her sloping nose and immediately went back to work. Rory was at home here. Brynne, on the other hand, had grown up here and still couldn't see herself as the owner. Taylor's Bookstore belonged to her mother, not her.

Just before Brynne let herself in to the restricted area of her apartment, she found a box on the landing.

"They delivered that about an hour ago," Nate called up.

"Thanks!" she said, stooping to pick it up.

Brides and Things, the return label read. Her heart went out of sync at the sight, screwing up her breathing. The wedding gods continued to mess with her head. Even her hands felt shaky holding it. All because her un-wedding dress had arrived.

She left the box by the door and headed back toward the bookstore, to Rory.

"Can we talk a minute?"

"For you, darlin', any time." Rory put the books she was organizing on the cart, giving Brynne her full attention.

"I know I'm being a broken record, but this is about Paul."

"The break-up?"

Brynne nodded. "He reminded me today how Mom loved him, and you did, too."

"Your mother absolutely loved Paul and was totally at peace with you marrying him."

"I was, too, back then, but since Mom died, I've lost that peace. I could use some Rory wisdom."

That made Rory laugh. "Like you ever took my advice before." She sat on a nearby chair, folded her hands in her lap and for a quick second, thought.

"Here's my take," she said. "Paul's a traditional kind of guy and you were raised," she paused as though searching for the right word, "untraditionally. Hell, you were practically raised in a bookstore by a couple of," she stopped briefly, "bookworms. Compatibility on the meaning of family was bound

to be an issue. I remember you two came to logger-
heads about kids." She glanced at Brynne for verification, and she nodded.

"As I recall you're of the 'kids shouldn't outnum-
ber the parents' way of thinking, and he's a 'more
the merrier' advocate. But the biggest and most important part is that you love each other."

"Can we back up a second? I'm actually stuck
at the motherhood part. I'm scared because I don't
know what motherhood will look like for me."

"And you expect a woman that's never had a
baby help you figure that out?"

They laughed, then things went quiet.

"Here's the thing," Rory said, "you can't wait to
overcome all your fears before you start living. So
it's up to you guys to work out the details, again,
but you've got to be straight with each other. Tell
him exactly how you feel, see where you can compromise and where you absolutely can't. Hopefully
that won't be a deal breaker."

"It makes so much sense when you put it like
that, but somehow I always muddle things up in
my mind when I should talk about it."

"Well, don't ever muddle this up. Remember I
love you, and I'll support whatever you decide. I'm
on your side, kiddo, and we'll be friends for life. I
hope that matters a little."

Brynne's eyes stung. A blurry vision of her mom
came to mind in her favorite flannel shirt telling

her the same, when Brynne had first told her about the engagement. She pulled Rory to standing and wrapped her arms around her honorary mom, trying her best not to cry. "Thank you, that means the world to me."

Chapter Nine

"Did you bring the dress?" was the first thing out of Eva's mouth when she opened the door of the rental.

"Of course!" Brynne held up the box. "Haven't even opened it yet. Thought I'd save it for the three of us." Surprising herself, Brynne had come up with the idea at her apartment. Since they'd picked it out together. She'd consider it another bonding session with her sisters. Or was the real reason she'd been procrastinating about looking at the dress because of what it represented?

Eva led the way across the family room, where Joe and Zack were roughhousing with the kids, Emma playing referee to their fake wrestling matches with Noah while keeping her eye on Estrella, who happily crawled in and out of the fray. A basketball game was muted on the extra-large flat screen mounted on the main wall. The visual caused a strange sensation in her chest.

Brynne waved and smiled at everyone as they made their way to the stairs and in return received the usual warm welcome. Both men jumped up and gave her a kiss on the cheek. Emma rushed to hug her around the waist, as though she'd known Brynne her entire short life. It was strange but endearing, and she found herself hugging the young one tight. Maybe this was how it felt to have a house full of kids, but it also felt like a room full of love.

Everyone already considered her one of the family, and she couldn't deny, the comradery was growing on her.

"We've reserved the master suite for the evening," Eva said, mounting the stairs, wearing a handkerchief-hemmed print dress in blue tones with a darker blue bolero-length sweater. Something Brynne would expect to see in the summer, not fall in Utah. But what could she expect from a person born and raised in Southern California, where, evidently, they had eternal spring as their weather forecast? She'd also expect to see such an outfit in a women's fashion catalog. Eva directed her up the stairs and two doors down to a bedroom big enough for a family of five, where Lacy nursed little Johnny while lounging on an enormous bed.

"If this isn't a good time…"

"Are you kidding? It's never a good time with this guy," Lacy said, looking down at the bump of head beneath a light yellow blanket, love written on her face.

"Don't even think of it. We've got refreshments and everything," Eva said. She walked to a portable three-tiered drink and food service cart. "We've got assorted crackers and cheese. Drink?"

The rental house apparently had everything a busy hostess could want. The thought amused Brynne, who hadn't a clue about hostessing. "What are you having?"

"I recommend the smoked gouda with wheat. Good pairing for taste. How about wine? There's a nice German Riesling here." She lifted the bottle and read the label.

With Brynne's usual experience when selecting wine being limited to house white or red, something from Germany sounded adventurous. "Sure. Might give me the courage to open this box."

"You haven't opened it yet?" Lacy piped up with an incredulous tone.

"You really are a terrible shopper," Eva said dryly as she opened the bottle and poured. "Are you afraid it will look gorgeous and you'll immediately want to get re-engaged?"

Brynne used the sudden burst of frustration to focus on tearing up the brown box to get to the dress inside.

"Wait, wait, wait! Did I just tick you off? I have

a way of being pushy," Eva said, finishing the pour and handing Brynne a glass, mid–cardboard rip. "Forgive me. If you're not ready to get engaged again, then I need to keep my mouth shut." But she didn't. "Lacy, you ready for wine?"

"In a minute. I'm almost done here."

Brynne inhaled and forced herself to calm down. Her throat suddenly felt closed up, and her shoulders ached.

Eva came back to Brynne. "And if you don't want to talk about it, as much as it will kill me, we'll understand."

Then Eva tapped her glass with Brynne's, and both took sips. Brynne pretended nothing was wrong, that she did this every day—visited people, quaffed wine and tried on wedding dresses for weddings that weren't officially rescheduled. Yet? But the dry white wine moved over her tongue with surprising hints of fruit, helping her relax a bit. At least Rory understood how she felt. Maybe her sisters could, too.

"Okay, let's see that dress," Lacy said with a curious gaze, giving Brynne the excuse to get right to the task.

Once the box was completely open, Brynne pulled out the off-white dress wrapped in tissue paper. As the dress unfurled, the tissues dropped to the floor.

"It's gorgeous," Eva confirmed her approval.

"Just like on the website. Try it on!" As Lacy

burped John, she watched the main attraction from the king-size bed surrounded by what seemed like dozens of fluffy throw pillows.

Brynne should have felt self-conscious stripping down in front of anyone other than Paul, but curiously she didn't, figuring, being triplets, they all had the same body with only the hint of individuality. She just hoped she wore hers well. Lacy, having just given birth, was way bigger on the top. Eva had a waist only daily crunches could produce. Down to her panties and bra, Brynne's defining feature was a three-inch scar on the right side of her lower abdomen from an emergency appendectomy at age fourteen.

"Wait a second," Eva said. "I've got that scar."

Brynne stopped cold in the process of unzipping and stepping into the dress. "You do?"

"I do, too!" Lacy said. "Late spring, when I was fourteen. It's all stretched out right now, thanks to the pregnancy, but it used to look just like yours."

"It will again, too, dear sister, have no fear. See, mine has gone back to the original size." Eva proudly displayed hers by lifting the handkerchief-hemmed dress for show-and-tell. "Same year, but summer."

"Wait, we've all had appendectomies?" Chills ran over Brynne's skin. "I was supposed to be a junior camp counselor that summer when I got appendicitis. That's crazy."

"Well, our bodies must be on the same time-line," Eva said.

"Is that possible?" Lacy asked.

Was that a medical thing? "I'm the nurse and I don't have a clue, but it does kind of make sense. Freaky but plausible."

Brynne quickly went back to donning the dress. Eva stepped in to help with the zipper. Then she moved back to let Brynne make a slow circular turn in front of the mirror.

Lacy sucked in a breath. "Looks more beautiful on you than that model at the website."

"I agree," Eva said. "It's perfect for you."

As usual they were being kind, because that was the way they were. But when Brynne looked in the mirror and saw the short white V-neck sheath with overlying blouson bodice covered in swirling beads and sequins, she had to agree. It was perfect for her. She turned to look at it from every angle.

"What about shoes?" Eva asked.

"I have the pair I bought for the wedding last March. Never could bring myself to return them. They should work."

"Good. And how will you wear your hair?" Eva playfully flipped Brynne's braid up in the air.

Brynne went still. "For what?"

"For when you get, uh, I mean wear it."

"This is a revenge dress, remember? Nothing more."

"But I thought we had it all worked out," Lacy

continued, disappointment obvious in her tone. Maybe a little frustration, too.

Which set off Brynne's. "You had it worked out? You mean I have to add your timeline to Paul's?" She'd been pushed to the limit on all sides and couldn't hold back her true feelings. "I feel like everyone's ganging up on me."

Eva waited for Brynne to take a breath, watching her carefully, then pursed her lips, thinking. "Oh, no, I'm so sorry! The last thing we want to do is upset you. But honestly, Brynne, the way you and Paul act around each other, we assumed your breakup was some little game you were playing."

"Are you willing to tell us what's really going on?" Lacy asked.

Brynne should feel beautiful in the pretty dress, but instead anger took over. Mom had taught her to always speak up for herself, to never let people run roughshod over her. "We have unresolved issues, and I can't move ahead until we've worked them out."

"Well, we certainly didn't know that part. From what Eva and I see, it's obvious you love Paul, and honey, if you can't tell how much he loves you, you need to start wearing glasses."

Brynne's hands sneaked toward her face and cupped her ears. "And therefore we should get married?"

"Again, forgive us for overstepping our bounds."

Eva narrowed her eyes and stared. "But why'd you buy the dress, then?"

"Like I said, to get back at Paul. He gave me free rein with his credit card, and I wanted to make him pay for giving me that ultimatum. We'd all just met. And, to be completely honest, it was a fun way to get to know you two." The explanation was all over the place and messed up, just the way she felt. About everything since Mom died. Since Paul gave her the ultimatum and especially since her two sisters showed up.

"With no intention to use it to get married in?" Eva continued to stare.

Brynne recalled being up front about that. Hadn't she? "I verified this dress could be used for other occasions, and you said yes."

The festive reason for the night had long disappeared.

"Look, I'm totally mixed up about getting married. Something just clicked inside when Mom died. As if it put a dark cloud on marriage. I haven't been able to get the enthusiasm back about the wedding since."

"What about Paul?" Lacy asked.

Brynne tried to unzip the dress herself. Eva's hand stopped her. "Stop. Just leave me alone. You just show up out of nowhere and start running my life. Everyone seems to be on Paul's side, and I'm…"

"Wait, wait, wait," Eva shot back. "No one is

out to get you. We're trying to help you get back on track. That's all."

"You don't know what's best for me. You don't even know me!" Could she sound more defensive?

The room went quiet. After a few seconds, Lacy began in a calm voice after she laid Johnny on the bed. "When my dad died—" she stood and walked toward Brynne "—I went to a grief group, and they told me how important it was to let out my anger." She put her hand on Brynne's arm, gently stroking her. "Sudden deaths do that—make people mad. Getting in touch with that anger is part of the process of letting go."

"And I was told by a counselor not to rush into anything," Brynne shot back, standing her ground. "Not to make big decisions." She made contact with Lacy's questioning gaze. "And it seems that's all everyone is asking me to do these days."

"I'm so sorry, Brynne." Lacy didn't flinch. "That's the last way we want to come off."

"Mom's gone. I'll never have her back." And they never had her at all, it occurred to her. They were wading into sticky territory.

"Paul wants to fix the situation by marrying me and moving on."

"That's what guys do. Tell him to stop. Ask him just to listen." Lacy seemed to have an answer for her every doubt.

"Honestly, I think I would have by now, but you guys had thrown my life for a loop, too." Sorry to be that way, but unable to stop herself, Brynne took off the dress and put her clothes back on in silence. It was awful being the one responsible for the thick tension that had descended in the room. She'd just insulted her sisters, which proved she had no clue how to be part of a family.

She avoided all contact until she was dressed and ready to leave. Completely aware of the dead silence, but trudging on, she left the dress with them, maybe as a reminder not to push her around, then said good-night, thanked them for the wine and left for home.

I've got a lot of thinking to do.

The next morning, as scheduled, Rory and Brynne rummaged through the one remaining cardboard box with more of her mom's papers and items, together at the small home Brynne had grown up in. After Mom had given Brynne the apartment at the store rent-free until she got her first nursing job, Rory had moved in to Brynne's old bedroom to help offset expenses. Or so they'd said. It had all seemed logical, and Brynne appreciated her independence.

Brynne had alienated her sisters last night and left under awkward and strained conditions. If they never wanted to talk to her again, she wouldn't blame them. The least she could do was help them with what they'd come to Utah searching for.

She and Rory had dealt with all the important papers and insurance policies after Jessica's death.

It had been a huge comfort having someone to go through it with, though, as usual, Paul had also offered to help at every point. This time she and Rory hunted for correspondences and personal items.

"Do you ever remember me getting a condolence card and some flowers from an aunt Allison?"

"Vaguely," Rory said. "We were both a mess around that time, though."

Brynne realized Rory was wearing one of Mom's old tops and wondered if that was comforting somehow. Then she remembered keeping a pair of Mom's favorite goofy socks. They had stacks of books all over them, and sometimes she still put them on. "Why did I throw out all the cards?"

"You didn't want to be reminded." Rory gave an understanding gaze. "It was a rough time."

"If I'd only known she'd possibly be a key to this puzzle."

"You didn't have a clue you were part of a puzzle yet."

"True." Brynne snapped her fingers. "What about our local florist? Wouldn't they keep a record of who sent flowers when?"

Rory's eyes brightened. "Great idea! I'll give them a call."

As Rory drifted into the kitchen to use a landline for the call, Brynne dug deeper into the box, coming up with nothing. In the background, Rory's slightly nasal voice queried the local shop owner. She sat back on her heels and sighed, her vision panning the room. Though evidence of Rory filled the room, there was still much of what Brynne had grown up with all around her. This had been her home since she'd been three years old.

Brynne noticed in the corner, on the second shelf of the bookcase, was a small stack of letters tied with a ribbon. Had they come from this box? Had they already looked at them, or had Rory separated them for a reason? Maybe Rory had forgotten to mention them, or maybe they had nothing to do with her mother, but Brynne was desperate. From sitting on her knees, she got up then took the few steps to reach the letters and cards. Rory continued with her interview in the other room. Untying the rose-colored ribbon, Brynne recognized her mother's writing, and her pulse quickened.

For Rory, the top envelope said. It was none of her business, but she missed her mother, longed to read her writing again and, on impulse, wanted to see the kind of birthday card she'd give her best friend. They'd always teased each other and loved to laugh together. It would probably be a funny card, sling some kind of insult, or general absurdity, and she could use a good laugh about now, remembering one more good thing about her mother— even though, growing up, Brynne had thought her mom's sense of humor was lame. With a deep hunger to bring a piece, any piece, of her mom back, she went for it.

Pulling the card from the lavender envelope,

she was surprised to see it was a frilly Valentine's card. *Odd*.

My dearest Rory,

She read on and caught her breath.

Everyone loves a good love story,
But ours will always be my favorite.
With all my love,
Jessica.

Brynne's heart stumbled over the next few beats as she reread the card. Friends said *love ya* or *hugs*, not…

Though she was off balance, with her ears ringing, she let the words sink in. *With all my love*.

She'd driven Mom and Rory to the airport a decade ago, dropping them off at the international terminal then watched from the car as they walked, arms around each other, ready for the biggest adventure of their lives. At twenty-one, she'd thought nothing of it. They were best friends, supporting each other. They were heading to France for the first time, and Brynne believed no one deserved a vacation as much as her mom and Rory.

Then, upon their return, Mom gave the newly available apartment above the bookstore to Brynne. She'd said it was about time her adult daughter had her own place.

Even though they'd kept separate bedrooms, it

became clear to Brynne that her mother and Rory were more than friends. She'd seen how Rory looked at her mother and how her mother passed secret glances back.

Though she was still breathless, her gaze slowly drifted over her shoulder toward the kitchen, where it had gone quiet. She found Rory, solemn-faced, watching her.

"Why didn't Mom ever come out to me?"

"Tell you we were involved? Lovers? Your mother had her reasons," Rory whispered, desperation in her glistening eyes.

Heat flushed from Brynne's crown to her stomach. "I pretty much always knew. But talking about something so intimate with Mom…"

Rory didn't move from behind the kitchen breakfast-bar partition. "And we live in a state that still doesn't recognize our kind of love."

"You could have moved to California."

"That's where your mom left, remember? The two people she trusted the most, her parents, turned their backs on her when she came out to them. It crushed her, Brynne. Changed her life. She wouldn't risk the same thing happening with you, the person she loved most in the world."

"But I loved her—nothing would change that."

"She had history you couldn't understand." Rory's guarded expression softened. "Besides, we didn't need California. We got married in Paris. Of course, it wasn't official, but nevertheless, we had a very romantic ceremony. Just the two of us." She leaned her elbows on the counter, lifting her right hand, lightly wiggling her ring finger. "We exchanged rings. And vows. That was enough for us."

The brightly colored, patterned cloisonné ring on Rory's right hand matched one Jessica had worn on a long silver necklace around her neck. It struck Brynne, *Mom had kept so many secrets.*

And Brynne had blindly accepted they were just a couple of middle-aged women sharing the mortgage to avoid facing the truth.

Brynne grabbed the bookcase to steady herself. How could they keep their love a complete secret all those years? "How could Mom be afraid I'd reject her? Because I wouldn't have. Never."

"It wasn't just you, honey. Like I said, it was a whole lot of other things."

Brynne made her way to Rory and hugged her long and tight. "All this time."

"Well, we always joked you had two moms." Rory tried to make light of a tragic situation but they wound up crying instead.

Later, as Brynne prepared to leave, still feeling dizzy over finally knowing what she'd always suspected, Rory grabbed her arm.

"I totally forgot to tell you, Allison did send a flower arrangement to the funeral home, but the shop clerk wouldn't share the return address or phone number. Something about not divulging personal information. I told her it was to send a belated thank-you card, and she said she'd check with the owner and get back to us."

Finally, a lead.

Brynne had a lot to apologize for to Lacy and Eva. But in all fairness, so did they. She'd been rude and angry and they'd been pimping Paul to her, so she left without hardly a goodbye last night. Now she also had one more huge revelation she wasn't ready to share yet. She knocked on their door with trepidation, expecting them to close it in her face.

Instead, "Hi," Zack said, his usual smile in place. "Come in."

"Are my sisters here?" Still shaken from that morning, she donned her big-girl panties and carried on.

Though a bit sheepish, both Eva and Lacy smiled when they saw her, and as soon as Brynne said the magic words—"I'm so sorry"—they joined in "We are, too" and they had a group hug.

"Can you forgive me?"

"We already have," Lacy was quick to add. "We talked about things last night and realized you were right. We showed up in town and immediately started acting like we knew what was best for you. Wasn't fair of us."

"Nothing can come between us now that we've found each other," Eva said.

With the unconditional love filling the room, Brynne smiled and fought back the misty eyes threatening to break free and sob. "That's not the only reason I'm here. I've found a lead."

"About us?" Lacy nearly squealed.

"Our birth?" Eva sounded more restrained, but she was obviously excited.

Brynne grinned, focusing on the mystery of them.

A half hour later, standing outside the Flowers Every Day shop, they made their final plans.

As a lawyer, Joe was happy to step in if the flower shop withheld Allison Roberts's phone number. But as the only *known* relative of the deceased Jessica Taylor, Brynne was in an awkward situation. "Why don't you know it?" the woman could ask. Then Brynne would have to face the shameful fact she didn't. It was just one more thing she'd have to take a long hard look at about living with *Mom*. Brynne's eyes drifted to the bright blue sky.

They stepped inside the cozy and cluttered store, hit right off by the overpowering scent of roses, then carnations. The fragrance got Brynne energized. Maybe they could finally get somewhere today. Fill in one of the many blanks.

Half of the shop walls were painted with morning glories and the other side of the room with wisteria. Vases and pottery sat on every conceivable surface of rustic tables and shelves, and in the back a bank of huge glass-doored refrigerators was full to the brim with assorted blooms.

Eva started with the line of questioning about

Aunt Allison, and when the woman hesitated, Joe came to the rescue.

"Why don't you call her and ask if she's willing to give us her contact information? It's really that simple," Joe said to the owner, Eva at his side, as Brynne and Lacy looked on. They held hands as tightly as she needed, which was apparently circulation-cutting tight!

"After getting the court to open your birth mother's health information, I forgot about other roadblocks," Joe casually commented as they waited for the clerk to make the call. "With the internet selling our personal information left and right, people are fighting back wherever they can," Joe added. "Maybe she doesn't want to be contacted."

"Then why send flowers?" Brynne couldn't for the life of her understand. "And cards at Christmas?" Why hadn't she ever thought to notice where "Aunt Allison" lived?

Lacy squeezed her fingers more, as if that was possible. "Something tells me we'll be able to make contact."

"I hope you're right." Brynne grimaced rather than whining in pain.

A few minutes later, the flower shop owner came back with a small piece of paper. "She agreed. Here you go."

Lacy let go of Brynne's hand to clap.

Brynne reached for the piece of paper, as though

it was golden. Her pulse raced as she read first the address in Santa Barbara, then the phone number.

"You've got to be kidding," Eva said. "That's where my house is—where Mom lives now that I'm living in Little River Valley. It's probably five miles away."

Brynne stared, taking in the random coincidence. A huge clue to the how and why of their separation had only been five miles away.

"Let's wait to call when we're alone," Brynne said, Eva and Lacy quickly agreeing.

"Tonight, after dinner," Lacy suggested. "After the kids are in bed."

"Works for me," Joe said. "Paul, Zack and I, plus the entire male Capriati clan, have plans to hang out at Mark's Tavern."

"First I heard of it," Eva mentioned.

"Guys' night out," he added.

Since it was the only pub-type bar in town, it made perfect sense.

They left the florist's, and as everyone set off in their own directions, having been given a time to show up at the rental later, Brynne was at loose ends. There was only one person she wanted to share the news with. She took out her phone and saw a missed call with a message from Regina James.

Regina James? The hospital nursing administrator? The reason for her call set Brynne's skipping through the next few beats. She missed her old job.

Sitting in her car, she returned the call, expecting to have to leave a message. After two rings the top nurse picked up, and Brynne introduced herself.

"Just the person I want to talk to. First off, I wanted to let you know it is coming up on six months for your leave of absence, and you will soon lose your seniority and longevity pay. And there is the matter of your accrued sick and vacation leave we need to deal with."

"Oh yes. I assumed I'd gone through all of my leave time."

"We need to know what your plans are."

Brynne's nerves took a dive to her gut. She'd expected as much, but was she ready to give up nursing for being a full-time business owner? Her stomach muscles clenched. "I understand."

"We gave you six months' leave, and well, it was tough filling your shifts, especially during summer vacations, and now with the winter holidays coming. And something else has come up. I'd like to have a meeting with you tomorrow if possible?"

"Uh, do you think it's necessary?" Probably an exit interview.

"It would be in your best interest," Ms. James said.

Why did she feel like she was about to get in trouble? She understood she needed to make up her mind once and for all—she couldn't leave her employer of eight years hanging forever. Or Paul? "Okay, yes. What time?"

"Nine?"

"I'll be there." Brynne hung up the phone, shaken and unsure. After everything she'd been through the past several days, this added push for a decision was overwhelming. Anxious and antsy, with her body crying out for peace, she speed-dialed Paul. She needed to self-medicate, and he, apparently, was her drug of choice.

"Is this your afternoon office time?"

"Every Thursday." He sounded happy to hear from her.

"Can you meet me at my apartment?"

"For *that* kind of office time?"

They'd been known to share an occasional afternoon tryst during his scheduled office hours after his classes on Thursdays over the past two years when she had the day off. With things being a bit rocky between them lately, she understood his need for verification.

"Um." With the excess frustration and anxiety she needed to work off, being with Paul sounded like the only way out. "Yes?"

"Be there in ten," he said. Had the man ever let her down? She smiled gratefully to herself, the swirl of anxiety circling her letting up just a bit for the first time today. But he'd hung up before Brynne had a chance to mention she wasn't currently at home. Which meant she'd have to hit the gas to make it there in time to meet him. As she drove like a demon, she knew Paul wasn't the only one tired of waiting for her to make up her mind. The hospital was, too.

When she arrived at the bookstore, Paul was chatting with Nate at the front desk, and she'd be lying if she didn't admit how happy she was to see him. He read the back of a book Nate must have handed him, so he was wearing his glasses. When he wore those studious frames, he always played into her secret fantasy about him. She dug making love to her professor! Her cheeks flushed, as they often did, at the sight of him. She may as well already be letting her hair out of the braid.

How obvious would it be, now, when she led Paul upstairs to her apartment? Nate might be young, but he was astute and extremely smart. They wouldn't exactly be fooling him. She shook her head—seriously, who cared? She was an adult and so was Nate. And Paul was the biggest, most well-adjusted adult she'd ever met. He glanced up from reading the book's dust jacket and smiled. Her heart seemed to shimmy.

Once inside the apartment, running from her past and future, she didn't waste a second launching into his arms for the first order of business on the afternoon's hopefully very, very busy agenda…

Later, curled around Paul and lying across his chest, in the semidark of the afternoon, after having equal parts stress, anger and blatant reassurance sex, Brynne put her head on his shoulder. With her hair damp from the strenuous workout with him, she knew beyond doubt she hadn't taken after her mother in that department. Control freak, maybe. "My mother was gay," she said, matter-of-fact.

Sublimely relaxed, he could barely lift his head. "I knew that."

Her head bolted upright. "How did you know, when I wasn't sure?"

"I just knew."

"Why didn't you tell me?"

"I assumed you knew, and we didn't need to talk about it, because it didn't matter to me or you. It was just who she was." Spoken like a man on the right side of a decision.

She rolled off him.

"They also looked lovingly at each other…a lot. And fought like cats! Ugh, *I* turned a blind eye."

"Maybe."

"What if she thought my love was conditional on her not being a lesbian, and that's why she never came out to me? That makes me sad. So, so sad."

Paul pulled Brynne to him, circling her with his arms and holding her close. He kissed her temple. "We may never know her reasoning for not telling you, but she knew you loved her—that's what mattered most."

His answer had to be number 110 of the reasons to keep him in her life. So why was she resisting his one, most important request so hard? Suddenly she knew one more thing for sure.

She needed Paul. Again.

Chapter Ten

Thursday night, as planned, Brynne showed up at the rental house, with a new onset of butterflies in her tummy. Was it possible tonight they'd finally get the information her sisters had been after for nearly a year?

"Can you hold Johnny for me?" Lacy asked, handing the swaddled bundle to Brynne the moment she stepped inside. "I need to brush Emma's hair. It's this thing we do, and, well, with everything going on lately, we haven't had a chance."

"Of course." How could Brynne refuse?

Lacy rushed up the stairs, and Eva was nowhere in sight. Probably tucking in her two little ones. Man, Johnny was tiny, and he had the cutest button nose. He sure had a lot of red hair, and his eyes shut tight like a porcelain doll. She cuddled him close, sniffed him. Fresh with the hint of spit-up. The thought made her smile. He squirmed and worked out some gas, which made her laugh. "It's tough getting the whole eating and pooping thing down, isn't it, guy."

Standing in the quiet living room, she thought of another house, the one Paul had wanted her so badly to love. It was a great house, she had to admit, but she kept holding on to her excuse—*it's still too soon.*

Tiny, ragged breathing sounds accompanied Johnny's head turn and search above Brynne's breast. "Sorry, little dude, I'm not your mother." Still, he felt so right, so sweet, so wonderful. Was she ready for the one at a time deal? The idea still caused a shudder.

After Eva and Lacy put their children to bed, since the guys were hanging out with Paul at the pub, the house was as quiet as a library.

"Before I make the call, you two should know something I suspected but finally verified this morning," Brynne began.

"Well, you've certainly piqued our interest," Eva answered.

"After all the surprises we've had lately, I can't imagine what else." Lacy played with the forgotten pacifier in her hands, waiting.

"Like I said, I had my suspicions, but this morning I found a love note from Mom, and Rory admitted she and Mom were lovers."

"Our birth mom was a lesbian?" Eva stated the obvious, wonder in her voice.

Brynne confirmed with a quick nod.

"I did *not* see that one coming," Lacy said, bewildered but not shocked.

Still baffled by the situation, Brynne was glad to have sisters to share the information with.

"So they were secretive about it," Eva said. "Why?"

"Rory was very guarded about everything. Part of the reason, she said, was they lived here, and marriage wasn't legal for them, and part was to protect me, evidently. Not now, but while I was in high school."

"And they just never got around to telling you?" Eva went to the sink and had a drink of water.

"Apparently."

Lacy got up from her place across the table, came around and hugged Brynne. "This isn't being sorry for you. This is about our birth mom never wanting you to know. It's so sad."

"I know. And confusing, because Paul said he knew, but it wasn't up to him to tell me, and it was never an issue for him, so why would it be for me?"

"Which it wouldn't have been, right?" Eva encouraged.

"Absolutely. Not at all."

"Oh, what a tangled web we weave, when first

we practice to deceive," Lacy quoted Walter Scott, quietly.

They sat in silence, studying each other, offering supportive smiles and tender glances. Brynne was struck by the melancholy mood setting in and didn't want to hijack the reason they'd come together tonight. The need to get to the bottom of their separation.

"Well, are we ready?" Brynne asked, getting out her phone as more butterflies flitted through her stomach.

"Wait! I don't have to nurse again for a couple of hours, so I can have a glass of wine."

"Then we all can, and I'm pouring," Eva jumped in. "If there was ever a time for wine, it's now. Red or white?"

"White," Lacy and Brynne said in unison, knowing their personal taste, and not DNA, directed the unanimous decision.

"That got my vote, too," Eva said as they chuckled over the irony.

Once fortified with half a glass of light and crisp vino, Brynne made the call, surprised that her hand trembled as she tapped in the numbers. The anxious stomach jitters from earlier seemed to have doubled. She put the cell phone on speaker mode and laid it on the coffee table. Then it seemed to ring forever, giving her time to take another quick sip of wine before an unfamiliar voice answered.

"Hello?"

"Is this Aunt Allison?" They'd agreed to start slow, admitting to one niece only.

Silence.

"I guess I should say my great-aunt Allison, since I believe you were my mother's aunt? Jessica Taylor?"

The woman sucked in air then swallowed. "Yes" was all she said on a breath. Almost as though she'd been waiting for this day as much as Lacy and Eva had, though probably a lifetime longer. Then, after a couple more seconds stretched on, she said, "Is this Brynne?"

Her heart soared with hope. Maybe the last piece of their puzzle would finally be solved. "Yes, may I call you Allison?"

"Yes."

"I'm so sorry I never got to meet you."

"Your mother was very private, but I should've come to visit. She did invite me on several occasions. Then, when she'd died, I simply couldn't face it."

That explained the no-show for the funeral, but what about all the rest? How should she bring up the main reason? Why hadn't they come up with a plan before making the call? Eva dipped her head eagerly, subtly urging Brynne on. Lacy popped an encouraging thumbs-up, eyes bright.

"The thing is, Allison, when Mom died, she left me with a lot of questions, and I was hoping you could fill me in."

"Oh, I imagine so. What would you like to know?"

Relief washed through Brynne. "There are so many questions. I'll try to keep them down to just a few, but I sincerely hope I can call you again sometime, too."

"That would be fine with me. I'd like that."

Wonderful! Lacy mouthed.

"My mother's best friend said we arrived in Utah from California when I was three years old. Do you know where we lived before that? Was it with my grandparents?"

"Oh no, honey. Not your grandparents. You lived with me."

"You? For three years?"

"More like four for your mother."

"In case you're wondering, we know Mom was a surrogate." Oops, she kept using *we*—would that make her aunt shut down?

"Okay. Yes. She was a surrogate. It was her way of setting out on her own. But the surrogacy didn't turn out like she'd planned."

Eva held up three fingers to emphasize the issue of three babies instead of one. Brynne took a breath, deciding to spit out the rest. "Some researching has been done, and I know I'm one of the triplets born that day. And, well, amazing as it sounds, we've found each other."

"You have?" The shock came through the speaker.

"Yes, and now my sisters and I are trying to figure out why we were separated at birth."

A long sigh ensued and clued them in how heavy on her heart the subject must have been. "So, you know," Allison said in a doleful tone.

"Only that we were separated, not why. But yes, we have found each other. Which is a completely different and huge story, but it's as though fate brought us all together."

"You should know that your sweet and dear mother was special, Brynne, very special. All she wanted was a chance for a new start. Your grandparents disowned her, and she had nowhere to go, so she came to me. I'm your maternal great-aunt, your grandmother's only sibling."

The quiet hesitation prompted Brynne to go first. "Why would they disown her?" She glanced at her sisters, who were holding hands and watching expectantly. Brynne was already sure she knew why. "I know that Mom was a lesbian."

The heavy inhale answered the question concerning Allison's pregnant pause. "Yes, and when she came out to her parents, they disowned her."

Brynne's heart broke again for her mother. Rory had told her they'd disowned her. Now it hammered the point home. No wonder she'd never told Brynne, when her own parents wanted nothing to do with her for being gay. "And that's why she moved in with you?"

"Yes, she was eighteen and lost. Didn't have a

clue what to do with her life. I don't think she'd even had a girlfriend yet. And college, without a support system seemed overwhelming to her. She got a job in the local Borders bookstore. She loved that job, too."

Now it made sense why Mom had always wanted to own a bookstore, or so she'd said.

"She wanted to set out on her own but didn't have a clue how to go about that, either. She'd obviously figured out she couldn't go far on a store clerk's salary. Then one day, she tells me she'd done some research on surrogacy, read a book about it from the store and thought she'd be perfect for it. But knew she had to wait until she was twenty-one."

Wow, Eva mouthed. Her mother, in all likelihood had been a virgin who was impregnated. With triplets. The thought was mind-boggling. All Brynne wanted was to have her mother there to hug and hold and cry with. Wow, what a life she'd had. And what secrets she'd kept.

"And did you know about the closed adoption?"

"Yes. The couple who wanted a baby—the man donated the sperm. But then she found out it was a multiple pregnancy, and she briefly thought about ending it when the sperm donor said he'd only bargained for one baby, couldn't afford taking more. But that couple wanted their baby so badly, and she was cleared healthwise to carry the multiple birth. She couldn't go through with ending it. Though I don't believe she'd told them there were three fetuses. Then the thought of separating the babies broke her heart, but her only other choice was to keep them herself, and both legally—because the sperm-donor father had his rights—and financially, she couldn't do that. It simply wasn't possible. So, with her back against the wall, she got the father to agree, and she scrambled to find two more families. But in the end she only found one. And since she'd only disclosed a multiple birth, not triplets, he must have thought she only carried twins. She never corrected him. Still separating twins was just as bad, but the adopting parents agreed to that stipulation. One baby each."

Silence hung in the air as everyone took in the burden and choice Jessica Taylor had had to make while so young. And the guilt the two adopting families must have carried. "Then she decided to keep me, the third baby?"

"It was a very difficult decision, and truthfully, she didn't have a choice. Not at all her plan when she'd agreed to carry a baby for someone else. But with the money she got, she could start a new life somewhere away from everything she needed to leave behind. Dear Jessica wasn't ready for the next issue, either."

She didn't have a choice. Brynne felt a sudden sense of not being wanted by her mother, though growing up, she'd never experienced a trace of that.

"There was another issue besides separating triplets?"

Another long sigh came through the speaker. "Being pregnant, carrying the babies, feeling them grow and move…she fell in love with her babies." Allison's words broke up, and she went quiet again, except for sniffing and throat clearing, while she found her voice. "The thought of giving any of you up broke her heart."

Brynne's eyes filled as deep sorrow invaded her. She glanced at her sisters, who reflected her reaction perfectly. They reached for each other's hands and all took a moment to recover. They didn't have to verbalize their longing and yearning all their lives for something they couldn't explain. They'd grown and developed together in the same amniotic sac—until they'd been separated. Oh, how her mother must have wondered every day of her life about the other babies.

"I wish Mom was here so we could thank her."

"She gave you life, but it was at great personal cost."

"I've always loved Mom, and now I think my sisters can forgive her and love her, too." With tears streaming down her cheeks, Lacy wholeheartedly nodded, while Eva looked on in agreement, though obviously overcome with the realization.

"Why did she live with you so long?" Brynne asked after several more seconds of silence.

"Poor child didn't know a thing about taking care of a baby and couldn't very well set off with a newborn. That's why she stayed with me after the delivery and saved up more money, while I helped with childcare. You were such a sweet baby, and I loved helping to raise you."

Brynne could imagine the smile in her words. Though it hurt thinking her aunt had never seen her after they'd left. And worse yet, Brynne had no memory of her.

"Such beautiful red hair, and the cutest smile."

Banishing judgment of any kind, Brynne took a moment to appreciate the gentle compliment. All the love and good intentions had only caused disconnection in three babies. Thankfully they'd found each other and could wipe that slate clean. But they'd never make up for their lost time.

"How did she choose who to keep?" Eva, always to the point, broke in. Allison probably couldn't even tell it was a different person.

"From what I was told, Jessica decided the first-born would go to the Winters couple, since they started the whole thing, and the second born to the single lady, Ms. Bridget DeLongpre. Whoever came out last would be hers. But please know she agonized over and cried buckets making that decision."

"I understand." Brynne could only answer for herself, but looking at her sisters' sympathetic expressions, she knew they agreed.

"The thing was, you, Brynne, were breech."

It seemed to be a life pattern, resisting, even while being born.

She also knew what that meant. "That explains why my delivery time was an hour after Eva's."

"Yes, after all that labor and delivering two healthy girls, she had to have an emergency C-section."

"Oh, poor Mom!"

What her dear mother must have gone through. Brynne knew firsthand Jessica's C-section scar had been gnarly due to the emergency, not a tidy bikini cut. Nope, it was a classic, right down the middle of her abdomen. That was most likely due to the need for a rapid delivery. Being third, Brynne had probably been showing signs of distress, due to the feet-first position. Natural delivery in that situation was dangerous, especially after her mother had probably been laboring for hours and hours.

All Mom had ever told her was she'd been breech. Now she knew the whole story.

Things finally made sense. Their mother had been in a tight spot—she'd been abandoned by her parents, rejected for admitting who she was. Then, trying something positive to give herself a future without depending on anyone, she was thrown another curveball. Triplets!

At an age when Brynne was still trying to decide what specialty in nursing she wanted to train for, her mother had had to decide the fate of three babies.

Chapter Eleven

After Brynne introduced Eva and Lacy to Aunt Allison, with her sisters making plans to meet the woman in Santa Barbara once they'd returned home, she ended the call. Her heart still pounded. To be honest, Brynne felt a bit left out with them all living within a short distance of each other and her up there in Utah.

Flabbergasted wasn't a strong enough word to describe their reaction to hearing their mother's tragic story, but they'd bonded tighter as a result. Having never imagined what actual sisterhood would be like, she fought the resentment creeping in. Her sisters were growing on her, and so was anger about her mother's decision to split them up. Though Brynne had forgiveness in her heart about

Mom separating them, beginning to understand the horrible predicament she'd found herself in, Brynne wasn't sure Lacy and Eva had come that far. Maybe after meeting Aunt Allison, they'd come around.

If they'd known what a strong woman and good mother Jessica Taylor had been, would they forgive her or be more upset? Even if they didn't forgive Mom, Brynne would understand why. Being closest, Brynne grasped Jessica's situation. She couldn't fault her mother for making the call on such a tough issue at twenty-one.

It finally sank in. Her life had changed and expanded in less than a week. She wasn't alone like she'd been feeling since her mother had died, either. She had sisters to depend on. Her own family.

Of course, Paul had been inviting her into his family since their first date. He'd also been outspoken about wanting his own. She'd been willing to compromise while Mom was alive. Now, with Rory and her sisters as backup, did she really have a reason not to?

"We have to check out on Saturday," Eva said, snapping Brynne out of her thoughts.

Reality hit her hard. They'd be leaving soon, and she'd only just discovered them.

"Zack's going to pick up the rental RV tomorrow afternoon," Lacy said.

"I see. Gosh, you got here so suddenly, now I can't believe you're already leaving." Was this really happening? They'd arrived without warning and would leave without Brynne being the least bit prepared. She was only now starting to get to know them, and soon they'd be gone.

"It stinks, doesn't it? Why don't you fly down for a couple days when we meet Aunt Allison?" Lacy continued.

"I guess that's a possibility." More things to consider, more changes to grasp.

"It won't be the same without the three of us."

Nothing ever would be again.

"That's why I was thinking of us girls having a girls only party tomorrow night," Eva said, waggling her perfectly shaped brows and looking ridiculous.

Brynne's brows scrunched down at the prodding, even while she held back her laugh. Sometimes Eva did the most absurd things, and because it seemed so out of character, it always made Brynne crack up. "Isn't an 'all girls' party for kids in their twenties?"

"Is it Utah or nursing that has made you so stuck in all these ways?" Eva seemed impatient, staring her down with those big, questioning, perfectly outlined eyes.

Brynne realized she absolutely could be a dud and was bordering on winning the title of least happy sister. "Okay, sounds fun. What do you have in mind?"

"We'll think of something," Lacy said, her eyes glinting mischievously. "Just leave it to us."

* * *

Brynne woke early Friday morning. After everything that had happened yesterday, one of the craziest days of her life, she'd gotten a late-night call from a slightly inebriated Paul when he'd gotten home from the pub, telling her he loved her and wanted to spend the rest of his life with her. She'd thanked him politely, hung up, then passed out. There simply wasn't one more thing she could've seen, said or done except sleep.

Now, at nearly the crack of dawn, her eyes popped open. She'd slept soundly and felt refreshed. A good thing. Her appointment with Regina James wasn't until nine. Still, she got up and made coffee. There was so much to sort out, and she'd barely had a moment to herself since her sisters had arrived.

She sat in the dim morning light in the kitchen, waiting for the coffee to finish. With the sound and wondrous scent of brewing, her thoughts ran free. She'd officially be giving up her nursing job today. Most likely having an exit interview. How did that make her feel?

Sick to her stomach. Sad. Wrong, all wrong. She loved her old job, only tolerated running the bookstore. What the heck was she doing letting her life's calling go?

The beep went off on the coffee maker, and she poured herself a cup, having learned over the years of being a nurse to drink it black while on the job. Grab and go, always keep a cup stashed near the bank of computers, her name in pen on the throw-away cup. There, at the electronic charts tables, she'd sip and chart her notes when time allowed. With her patients content, treatments and meds given, she'd always found those moments a reward for working hard and pulling off another shift.

Taking a drink of hot coffee, she remembered how she'd also gotten used to consuming it luke-warm and cold on the job. Most days were nonstop, and eight years was nothing to sneeze at. Was she really going to give it all up?

Truth was, she missed being a labor and delivery nurse. She'd loved helping to birth babies, dealing with both healthy and complicated pregnancies and deliveries. It occurred to her that in the last couple of years she'd even assisted with a surrogate preg-nancy or two. Wow—she'd had no idea how sig-nificant that was to her until now.

She'd always thought nursing would be the job she'd have for the rest of her working life. Then life changed. Radically.

Last spring, before her planned but never-to-be wedding, she'd believed she could have it all. The marriage to Paul, the house, the job, the…kids? That had always been the one sticky part for her, the kids. Her only experience with babies had been part of a job. A job she loved.

For Paul, the issue had been how her job often seemed to run her life instead of the other way around. She liked the challenge of finding time together. He always wanted more.

Funny how as an L&D nurse she'd never truly allowed herself to think about having her own babies. She'd always held the sacred act of giving birth at a safe, professional distance. Not something for her, but for others. It was a job. How many times had she participated in patient births? Too many to count. Her resistance to babies had nothing to do with seeing so many women brave through that sometimes-treacherous thing called labor, either. Well, maybe a little. She'd seen both smooth and horrendous labors. Some enough to make her eyes pop out, leaving her wonder if she could willingly put herself through it.

Then, not even a week ago, she'd been dragged into the most amazing birth of her life—Lacy's emergency delivery. And the last couple of times she'd held Johnny, something had stirred inside. For the first time ever, instead of wondering if she'd treat her own kid like a job, she'd felt what could only be described as an inkling of maternal instinct.

And Paul had sure made it clear how much he wanted children before they'd planned the wedding.

Wow. Life continued to spin in new directions, which was a challenge for a certified control freak. But it was also an opportunity to choose her path. Make a stand for her life, and with whom she wanted to spend it.

Maybe it *was* now or never, as Paul hinted.

She finished her second cup of coffee and headed off to shower. There, under the full blast of dual showerheads pounding her back, she understood how she'd always assumed giving birth, having a family, that kind of happiness was for other people, not her.

She lathered and rinsed then washed her hair. Turning her face toward the hot water, the reality of having a baby with Paul, maybe more than one, hit her between the eyes. Could she handle such a thing without Mom as backup? Would Paul be her anchor now? Would she be expected to do all the bending or would he consider a compromise?

She turned off the water and wrapped herself in a towel. Gooseflesh covered her skin and she blamed the cooling fall Utah weather rather than her thoughts. She blow-dried her hair, French braided it down the back and slipped on black pants and boots and a long-sleeved light blue sweater, then grabbed her all-weather jacket and headed out the door.

Brynne arrived at the hospital nearly forty minutes early for her appointment, wanting to avoid any of her fellow nurses. She was still too raw from everything else going on in her life—having to deal with this life change, finally giving up her job on top of it, hit her hard.

She'd needed time to understand how the bookstore worked. Rory had been a big help, but Brynne needed to make it hers. In honor of her mother and all. She would've thought having grown up and around the store, it would've been second nature. But not so. Sometimes she felt she was forcing her mother's dream onto herself. And truthfully, it wasn't a perfect fit. She was able to admit that now.

She hid out in the human resources department in the basement. Not wanting to look suspicious while loitering, she read the job listings posted on the wall. There were several per-diem RN jobs, some float positions, not at all of interest to Brynne, and one or two in the L&D department. Well, that had some merit. If she was looking. Which she wasn't.

Besides, per diem would never account for steady work, was only meant for someone wanting part-time nursing hours and who didn't mind an irregular schedule. The best of both worlds?

Hmm, full-time and part-time jobs galore were also available. What was going on? She had no business being so interested in nursing jobs. *Just killing time, remember?*

Oh my gosh, there was her job posted for those already employed at the hospital. After two weeks it would go out to the public if no one from inside had applied. She wasn't ready to let it go, but she had a responsibility to her mother. The bookstore had been left to her, and it couldn't run itself.

All those years Jessica Taylor had put her heart and soul into having her own bookstore, and it meant so much more now. Aunt Allison had opened her eyes to the significance. She couldn't let her mother down.

But dammit, her heart wasn't in it!

Brynne checked her watch—fifteen minutes to nine. She left HR and headed for the basement elevator. When it arrived, she pushed the third-floor button, then, after the doors opened, she turned left toward the administration offices. *Bye-bye, job.*

Regina James sat behind a large desk covered with papers and files and Post-it notes in a rainbow of colors. Her tawny beige skin and jet-black hair were highlighted by her white nurse jacket.

Regina's smile brightened the room when Brynne entered and sat. Though her stomach had taken flight again.

"It's so good to see you. How have you been?" From happy one moment, to a split second of concern, Regina's expression did quick calisthenics in the exchange.

"I'm doing well. Thank you for asking." Brynne recited her reflex reply.

"We know you've been through a lot these past several months." With beautiful skin, the only thing giving away Regina's nearing retirement age was a slight yellow tinge to her eyes. "But it is time to clear up your status."

"I saw the listing downstairs."

"Your job? That wasn't supposed to go up until after I talked to you."

"It's okay." She fiddled with her fingers in her lap. "I'm still not ready to come back."

"That does bring me to the other reason I asked

you to come in today. Now, I know you've just said you're not ready to come back today, but maybe in a month or two?" She waited for Brynne to react, but Brynne was confused and unsure where the conversation was going. Not wanting to commit to anything she'd regret later.

"The reason I say that is because Beverly Unger is planning to retire in a couple of months."

"My supervisor?"

"Yes. And when we asked Beverly who she thought would be a good replacement, she wasted no time in saying you!"

"Me?" Brynne was beginning to sound weak even to herself.

Regina nodded patiently.

"She said you've pinch-hit for her a number of times when she was on vacation, and she feels with the proper training, you'd be perfect for the job. The staff likes you, and you know how the department works." Regina put down her pen and sat back in her chair. "Truth is, we'd rather hire for this position from the inside, and there are a few people we'd rather not have apply."

Lazy Kris, who knew how to cut corners and do as little as possible during her shift being one of them? Samantha, on the other hand, a long-term employee, an excellent RN and easy to work with, would be a great choice. As she remembered, Samantha's daughter was nearing college age, and surely, Samantha could use the bigger income. But would she want all the responsibility that came with it? Would Brynne?

"We'd rather offer the job to you right off to avoid hurt feelings from others on staff. What do you say?"

If it had been seven months ago, Brynne would've jumped at the chance. She loved her job, but having a professor boyfriend had influenced her to want to improve her status, too. To move up the ladder of success. Paul had big plans to take over his department—why shouldn't she? They'd be two professionals juggling the responsibilities of work and family together. If any man was up to that task, Paul was.

The question remained, was she? She knew she was qualified and could do the job, and was glad admin felt the same, but the offer had come at the worst possible time. "May I have some time to think about this?"

"Is a week enough?"

In the last seven days, with her sisters showing up, Brynne knew firsthand how life could change on a dozen levels, and this weekend was still completely up in the air. Would a week be enough? "Could you make that two?"

Regina offered a conciliatory smile. "If that's what you need to make up your mind. Absolutely."

"Thank you."

Regina opened the calendar on her computer.

"Let's say same time, nine? Two weeks from today?"

With new jitters in her stomach, Brynne agreed to the plan, even while having no clue what the outcome of those two weeks would bring.

As she left the meeting, one thought stuck in Brynne's mind—why was life delivering all this goodness at once?

Then another idea popped into her head. It was about time to start spreading around some of that goodness.

Brynne entered the bookstore to find Rory working busily on a display of this month's bestsellers. All the big author names were represented on hardback books and arranged for the customers to see the moment they walked in. Rory smiled as she worked, and Brynne knew immediately she'd made the right decision.

"Hi," Brynne said as she sidled up to the display.

"Hey." Rory looked up.

"Slow day?"

"Not at all. Just sold a bundle of books."

"The lady who comes first thing every month for her category romances?"

"Yup. She bought all six."

"As usual."

"Plus Nora Roberts's newest hardback."

"Great." Brynne looked in the near vicinity, finding no one within earshot. "Um, you have a minute?"

Rory glanced around at the near empty store. "For you, always."

Brynne took that as her cue to give the woman she was about to lay a huge surprise on a big hug. Rory accepted it like a woman who needed a hug, too, so they lingered a bit. Then Brynne waited for Rory to look up once she'd let her go. "You've never once complained about something, and I think it's time that we make things right."

Rory looked confused.

"This store." Brynne opened her arms and glanced around the well-kept though aging place of business. "It should belong to you, not me."

"But you're Jessica's daughter."

"The store came to me by default because Mom didn't have a will. You and I both know that. But it rightfully belongs to you, her partner, her best friend. Her wife." She hadn't expected to get emotional, but saying it out loud—that her mother had had a significant other who loved and missed her—hit her hard. "You, should've automatically gotten this business, not me."

"But it's your family business."

"And no one was more family to Mom than you. Rory, I have a profession. My heart is in nursing, and I realized today that's what I want to go back to. I've been offered a job, and I think it's the right direction for me."

Rory's hands flew to her cheeks. "I'm not sure I can handle this alone."

"Then make Nate full-time!"

Rory obviously liked the idea; as she nodded a few tears escaped the outside corners of her big brown eyes.

"I've got a brother-in-law who's a lawyer. I'm sure he'll be glad to walk us through whatever process is necessary to put this business in your name."

They hugged each other again, and it gave Brynne courage to meet Paul and tell him her big plans.

It was Friday at the university, which meant the grilled-cheese truck would be there. Brynne texted Paul and met him for lunch on campus, though her stomach was tied in a knot and no way would she be able to eat the whole thing.

They ordered then strolled around while waiting for pickup. After giving him the rundown on her morning, she went for it—the news out of left field.

"Anyway, they want me to take over the L&D supervisor position." She watched him carefully for his first and honest reaction.

He stopped midstep, his mouth left open, his eyes and mind obviously working out the information. "Is this something you want?"

"Honestly, I'm not sure yet, but I've got two weeks to figure it out." She beamed, sensing the huge opportunity being handed to her. An advancement, because they believed in her. She'd oversee something important—the labor and delivery department. But that tiny voice quickly registered a complaint—*bookstores are important, too.* But she knew clearly now, that was her mother's dream, not hers, so she'd passed it to Rory. Nursing was her calling.

Their order got called, and after picking their sandwiches up, they found a bench under a white myrtle tree and sat. In Paul's defense, he was obviously trying to be supportive about her announcement, but his smile, the happiness he tried to showcase, didn't ring true. Something was wrong.

"What?" she said, opening her sandwich wrapper.

"It's just—" he put his on his lap "—I thought you loved the hands-on part of nursing. Wouldn't this be all administration stuff? Schedules, meetings, you know. The opposite?"

She sighed her impatience, letting his truth hang around her neck like a bowling ball on a chain. He knew her so well that he'd already caught on before she had. He could be so irritating. She tore off a bite and chewed hard.

"Is that really what you want?" he repeated, which ticked her off, like she didn't know her own mind. Except she'd been asking herself the same thing the entire drive over.

He studied the melted cheese seeping from between the lightly browned slices of sourdough. "We always had enough trouble making our schedules work when you worked the wards, then the bookstore seemed to take every ounce of your time and energy. Now, administrative work—wow, we'd never see each other."

"You just turned my good news to being all about you." Heat rose up her neck, into her cheeks. Was he being a jerk about this on purpose?

"That's not what I meant to do."

"It's what you didn't say that ticks me off. I'm sure this isn't part of your vision for us. Me being as busy as you with an important job. Who'll hold down the homestead? Am I right?" The log cabin popped into her head.

He gave a flat look, not denying her statement. She knew him as well as he knew her, and his vision for them was far more traditional. As in his mother and father's generation. They'd supposedly hashed all that out the first time around, when planning their wedding.

"I just said it's what I want." She doubled down, even though the opportunity wasn't exactly what she wanted, but in the ballpark. "So where does that leave us?"

Her sisters, Paul—no one had said it out loud, but the pressure was on her to caravan with the new in-laws to Las Vegas Saturday afternoon. Why? Well, obviously to finally do the deed that had been aborted when Mom had died: tie the knot.

Enough with the grieving, they all seemed to hint. *Move on!*

Right now, that knot felt more like a noose. They

stared at each other over grilled-cheese sandwiches in a standoff.

With sudden and deep sadness, she sensed Paul had finally realized they might not be compatible on what they wanted out of life.

"You're right. Of course, you are," Paul said. "It shouldn't be you who has to make all the sacrifices. I'd never want to hold you back."

"But…" She'd give him enough rope…

"Honestly, I don't think this job is what you really want or even need."

That lit her already fizzing fuse. "Look, I need and want whatever I say I do. Get it?"

His eyes fired back at her with a look she'd never seen before. "And I get to decide when it doesn't work for me. It seems more like a recipe for disaster, another one of your 'I'm doing this because I said I would' decisions. How'd the bookstore work for you?"

Oh, he was fighting dirty. She gripped the fingers on her free hand tight.

"But I don't want to hold you back," he quickly added.

"So you think I'm making the wrong choice?" After everything he'd put her through this past week, he was giving her an out? He didn't want to "hold her back." Hell, no, she wouldn't fall for that. This was about him and what worked or didn't work for him.

Before reality came crashing around Brynne,

she tore a page from her anger book. Squinted her eyes, shook her head, letting him know how he'd pissed her off.

Paul was right, damn him! It really wasn't her dream job. But why couldn't it be? If she'd been more secure in her reasons for wanting the job, she'd fight him about his being a traditionalist.

Without another word, she stood, leaving the uneaten sandwich on the bench, and walked away, leaving Paul still holding his, with a whole lot to think about.

Everything in the life she'd known up until six months ago had changed. Radically. Now she'd add one more. The only thing her so-called great news had accomplished was blow up their future.

"Brynne?" he said softly.

She pretended not to hear, though he called out several more times.

Late Friday afternoon, the last thing Paul wanted to do, after his dismal lunch with Brynne, was hang out with Zack and Joe again. But Zack had called and asked for a special favor. To meet him and Joe. And they were both great guys, ones he'd hoped to have as brothers-in-law. Though now, after saying all the wrong things at lunch, he was positive Brynne would never marry him. Well, these guys could still be his long-distance friends, at least.

Bringing a load of sadness with him, Paul showed up at the address Zack had given on the phone. It was on the outskirts of town, one of the city's super homes. The kind only wealthy transplants from tax-laden Western states could build or buy.

He whistled through his teeth as he got out of the car. Then, he saw the RV. "Holy sh—" Paul said just as he spotted Emma and stopped himself.

"I know, right?" Zack said, greeting him with a thump on the back. "Big rig."

"This is so exciting!" Emma said with her usual enthusiasm about everything in life.

He wished she'd rub off on him and Brynne. "Thirty-six-footer?" Paul asked, hoping to sound knowledgeable but knowing squat about such things.

"Right around there." Zack tucked Emma to his side with his arm around her shoulders. Her eyes were wide, taking in the behemoth motor home like it was Christmas on wheels.

"How'd you find it?"

"Eva's favorite way to do business," Zack said. "Internet. RV share. Same way she found the house."

"The guy probably uses this RV once a year," Joe broke in after a friendly knuckle knock with Paul. "Rents it out the rest of the time. Makes big bucks, too."

"Those who have get more," Paul said under his breath, aware how cynical he'd become since lunch.

"There's only one problem with our plan," Zack said, ignoring the prior sarcasm, and gazing hope-fully toward Paul, who felt the opposite of Mr. Sunshine. "We need someone to drive it back here after we get home, and I'm hoping you're the man. You interested in taking a quick trip through Vegas and beyond this weekend?"

Paul had never driven anything so big—would he even be able? But a shot at hitting the road in pure luxury still managed to pique his downtrodden interest. All that power and magnificence under his control. What guy wouldn't want the chance? "How would that work?"

"Well, Joe and Eva will drive my car back home while I drive the RV. You'd have to come all the way to Little River Valley, but you'd get a free ride home, on my dime for doing me the favor of returning it."

"What would I do with my car?"

"I've asked for a tow-bar attachment, so you can tow four wheels down."

Paul wasn't exactly sure what that meant, but figured he'd find out, so he nodded like he understood.

A broad-shouldered and wide-girthed fellow who looked like a retired linebacker from the NFL approached from the grand house. "Gentlemen, I'm Ben," he said in an unexpectedly high voice. "Which one is Zack Gardner?"

Zack, with Emma tagging along, stepped away with the man after a quick introductory handshake, presumably to handle the business part of the RV-share deal. Instead of worrying about whether he could drive this rig—which he was surprisingly eager to find out under the current circumstances—

Paul took the time to grill Joe over the thing foremost on his mind.

"May I ask you something?"

"Of course."

They stood side by side, the comfortable way for guys to talk, staring at the RV instead of each other, which also helped Paul bring up what he needed.

"With you being the mayor and Eva running a nonprofit, plus two kids under three, well, how the hell do you do it?"

Joe flashed him a quick look and grinned, showing almost all his straight white teeth. His olive-toned skin plus the late-afternoon golden sun made everything more pronounced. Paul went back to assessing the RV.

"It's a circus, but a great circus. We just work it out. It's not easy, but at the end of the day I know I get to go home to the most beautiful woman in the world and two of the greatest kids a guy could ever want." Joe flashed that smile again. Paul caught it in his peripheral vision. "Eva can work from home, and often I walk into chaos. House a mess, dirty diapers, kids crying, Eva with every hair out of place."

"Not Eva!" Paul turned to Joe briefly for verification, though half teasing.

"Oh yes. That's the down and dirty of it. But I still love it."

"But she works from home and that helps, right?"

"Theoretically. She has a lot of responsibility with Dreams Come True. She also has help come in to watch the kids when she does interviews on-line or takes appointments with her clients. Can't depend on the kids napping at the same time." Joe stroked the two-day growth on his jaw, thinking. "But when I come home and those kids look at me like I'm Santa Claus, every day, and Eva lets me know how glad she is to see me with a kiss hello? There's nothing like it. All worth it. Then I'm on duty, which is probably why I get that welcome kiss. She gets a break. Like I said, a nonstop circus."

That was how Paul had always imagined his life would be with Brynne—beautiful chaos—but he wondered what Eva's side of the story would be. Still, from what he'd seen of Eva and Joe, they were obviously in love and extremely happy together. Something they worked hard at. That was the key to a solid marriage. Compromise and hard work. His parents had done it, though his mother had made most of the concessions by working part-time as a Realtor. Brynne was happiest as a nurse, not a bookstore owner. She knew it now. And it was up to her to figure out what the right job was, not up to him to presume to know better. If he could have a redo of lunch, he'd just keep his mouth shut and be happy for her.

They spent the next few moments kicking tires and pressing on the frame of the motor home, open-ing things, looking under others. Their talk was over.

Brynne wanted what she wanted, with the opportunity at the hospital, and he wanted his old dream—marriage and a family. At what cost? They both needed to give up something for the greater good, and so far he hadn't budged. If running the L&D department made Brynne happy, he didn't want to be the guy holding her back.

Having figured out his end, he reached into his pocket for his cell phone to call and tell her. After the tense afternoon he'd spent, he needed immediate gratification. But he'd probably be a jerk and say something stupid, like, "You can do any job you want as long as I get to marry you. We'll work the rest out as we go along."

Fortunately, he didn't get the chance to foul up again. Zack and the RV guy came back to where the rig was parked, having finished quickly with the devil in the details part. Zack dangled the keys and fob with a victorious grin. "Now that I've signed my life away, let's try this sucker out."

"Let me show you a few things first," the linebacker, Ben, said. "As I said, it can sleep up to eight."

They unlocked the door, and one by one each person stepped inside, where they found a small but upscale apartment. Whitewashed wood floors, a mounted TV above an electric fireplace. Crafted woodwork and cabinetry throughout, overstuffed leather sofa and dining nook on one side, two oversize loungers in the same upholstery on the other, which sat next to a mini kitchen with stainless steel appliances, trendy gray backsplash and white quartz countertop. *Man, oh man.*

From where Paul stood, the first bedroom was on the other side of the TV/fireplace partition, keeping an open concept by forgoing a bedroom door. At the end was a surprising-sized bathroom. This was nuts!

"Look, Dad, I can make lunch for you and Lacy while you're driving!" Emma practically danced in front of the kitchen area. "And I can watch movies? Can I?"

Zack nodded patiently at his daughter while checking everything he could think of, turning things on and off, testing the sliding panels that increased the indoor width enough to dance in or host a small cocktail party. Paul had never seen anything like it. And he was supposed to drive this rig home from Little River Valley to Cedars in the City? Preferably with Brynne by his side. Hey, they could have a mini vacation on the way back. Spend a few days at a place he'd heard about near the Hearst Castle called Cambria, then take their time going home from there. Of course he'd pay for the extra days, miles and gas on his end. That was, if he could talk Brynne into coming along this weekend. Maybe he'd even get the nerve to pop the question again.

There he went, making plans without Brynne's input. Would he ever learn?

"Paul?" Zack broke into his deep thoughts.

He shook his head. "Oh, sorry?"

"I said, what do you think? Will you be able to handle this?"

"Do I need a special license?"

"No special class driver's license needed for personal-use RVs," the linebacker owner recited in textbook form.

"I could live here!" Emma piped up, making everyone smile.

Paul probably could, too. But only if Brynne was by his side. "I could, too." He needed to be positive about something first.

They filed out one by one. An idea popped into Paul's head about checking out the driver's seat, and he turned to go back up the stairs, forgetting he was second to last. Ben was right in front of him. When he quickly about-faced, the man had just finished adjusting his ball cap, and his elbow came down hard directly into Paul's right eye socket.

Pain shot through his eye and nose, and soon there was blood.

"Oh, so sorry," Ben said, looking horrified.

"My fault." Paul held up his free hand while holding back the bloody nose with the other.

Joe was quick to hand him a handkerchief. Who even carried those anymore? He gratefully took it and, concentrating on his nose, he pinched below the bridge above the bleeding nostril.

"Oh man, you're gonna have a shiner," Zack warned. "Is there ice in that refrigerator?"

Continuing with the horrified expression, Ben

nodded and pointed. Zack flew up the stairs and came back with a baggie full of ice. Paul gratefully took it and placed it over his nose and right eye, aware the lid seemed swollen already.

Fifteen minutes later, looking like the guy called Mayhem on that TV commercial, Paul took the wheel of the RV. Zack had taken pity on him and given him first dibs on trial driving around the block. With a wad of tissue up one nostril, he quickly forgot his black eye. Because this baby drove smooth!

Chapter Twelve

Only because it was Eva and Lacy did Brynne agree to the girls night out. Because she had no intention of going to Las Vegas and they'd be leaving soon. She was still mad as hell at Paul for his "I don't think that's what you really want" attitude about her new job offer, so maybe it would help her mood, too.

She brought the special wedding shoes as instructed. They would've hounded her unmercifully if she hadn't, since they had the dress she'd forgotten in a snit the other night. They'd probably expect her to try it on again tonight at some point. Shoes and all.

She'd just play along, because after tomorrow

they'd be gone, and who knew when she'd see them again?

"First off," Lacy said the instant Brynne walked through the door, "we're sorry with all our hearts we upset you last night. We got carried away and didn't consider your feelings."

"Look, I've been a PIA the whole time you've been here. I'm sorry, too. It's just a crazy time right now."

"Tell us about it!" Eva said, not letting Brynne wallow in her situation for even a second. "Everyone's lives have changed. There's no going back."

Oh, but there was for the on-again, off-again wedding plans. Which were currently off. For good. For the sake of her sisters and their fun night out, she wouldn't bore them with the details.

"Okay, let's get this over with," Lacy said. "All forgiven? Group hug."

A second later, Lacy reached behind her and produced a silver plastic tiara with huge pink glass jewels.

"You have to wear this tonight. It's Emma's, and apparently she doesn't travel without it. She said you could borrow it."

Brynne screwed up her face at the suggestion and winced when Lacy poked the tiara through her hair. "That's sweet of her?"

"You may think this is dumb," Eva said, "but Lacy and I have gone back and celebrated every single birthday we missed together, and now it's your turn to do some hyperspeed catching up."

Brynne might be in the dumps, but she wasn't a total dud. Her sisters didn't have anything to do with her current state of affairs, and they didn't deserve her sour mood on their last night together. She'd seen the huge recreational vehicle parked in the driveway on her way in. They were checking out tomorrow by noon and planned to drive home. All of them!

It could be months before she saw them again.

Her heart ached at the thought, surprising her, but she couldn't deny it. Two bright-eyed sisters stared at her, waiting for her to shape up. Brynne owed it to them not to wallow. "Then let's do this thing," she said, adjusting Emma's tiara.

Eva and Lacy grabbed their purses after saying goodbye to Zack and Joe.

"I've reserved the small private banquet room at a place called Madeline's Wine Bar and High Tea Room. Nice pairing," Eva said on the way out, obviously impressed with the colloquial way things were done in Cedars in the City. "By the way, they serve more than wine if you ask nicely." She winked before they met the Lyft waiting at the curb and got inside.

Brynne had conveniently left the wedding shoes back at the house, and she was relieved to see they'd both forgotten the dress. They wouldn't have expected her to try it on again, this time with the shoes and tiara, at the wine bar, would they? Didn't matter anyway, because she had zero plans of ever wearing that dress.

"Here," Lacy said, after they were safely ensconced in the cozy banquet room at the wine bar, the tables set for high tea and spirits. The historical British wallpaper and decorations added to the atmosphere. She handed Brynne a red sash, obviously makeshift, with glittered wording—Bad Influence, but Hot.

As if! Brynne couldn't help but guffaw at the accusation. "I think Lacy's the one who should wear this."

"Nope," Eva said, giving Lacy her own sash, which said, Hot Nursing Mama.

Brynne shook her head, grateful to have her sisters to pull her out of the funk. But when Eva donned her sash—which stated, Hot Mess—she wanted to trade.

If that wasn't the truth, nothing was. This was never the way Brynne's life went. Ever!

Her annoying tiny voice piped up—*High drama is kind of fun sometimes.*

It'd certainly gotten her a lot of extra time in the sack with Paul this week, though she was *still* mad as hell at him.

With tiny appetizers lined up on the usual tea cake and sandwich stands, and chilled wine ready to pour, the sisters got right to the business of indulging and enjoying themselves. Truth was, Brynne couldn't think of two people she'd rather have a going away party with.

"Mmm," Lacy said, licking her fingers. "Try those little salsa and cheese tortilla cups."

"The gouda cheese on cucumber slices is good, too," Eva said, loading more onto her traditional British-patterned bone-china appetizer plate.

Brynne went directly to the mini quiches wrapped in bacon and wasn't disappointed. And everything seemed to go great with the white wine. "This is the best wine I've ever tasted," Brynne said, half a glass in.

"California's finest," Eva said.

"You two can plan my parties any day," Brynne said, immediately sensing the irony coming from a person who had never once thrown a party. Except for her mom on her fiftieth, only three short years ago. The usual grieving thoughts forced their way in, and if she didn't consciously work to push them out of her head, they could ruin the fun. Fortunately, tonight, dressed in the armor of a tiara and party sash, she was able to scoot the downers right out of the room. "Hand me one of those canapé thingies, please," she asked Lacy, who quickly obliged.

Taylor Swift played through the banquet room speakers, and it was no shock when Eva got up and danced like a diva. Why wasn't that on her sash? Brynne got up and joined her. Though much clunkier. And it still felt good.

"Wait!" Lacy said, taking a picture of them, then

pulling a large cardboard sign from her oversize tote. "This is for your mug shot." She handed the black card with white print to Brynne, who read it quickly before agreeing to hold it up and frown for a picture. *Bridezilla. Crime: Cold Feet.* And underneath, a long line of inmate numbers, which looked suspiciously like her birthday and Sunday's date? Wait a second, was this a girls' night out party or a bachelorette thing? She'd never been to one but had seen movies about them.

Trying to be a good sport, Brynne let Lacy snap several pictures, thinking, *If the mug shot fits...*

"Perfect," Eva said, closing the door so they could have more privacy. The room provided several comfortable chairs to recline in while they drank, chatted and ate more.

As they relaxed, certain questions came to Brynne's mind. "You're not planning to bring a stripper in here, are you?"

"No!" Lacy ricocheted her answer.

"Do they even have strippers in Utah?" Eva couldn't help herself.

"Okay, good, because I'm starting to enjoy myself."

They ate and drank more. "How'd you guys meet Zack and Joe?" She'd been meaning to ask them all week but hadn't had a chance until now.

Eva shot Lacy a look. "You go first."

Lacy took a sip of wine and stared off in the distance. "I actually first met Zack when I was twelve.

He was a construction guy on his first job, and I'd had to go to work with my dad and his food truck because Mom had died earlier that year." Briefly, Lacy's eyes glistened, but she put a quick stop to it. Brynne wasn't the only one who'd lost a mother. "Anyway, I knew he was the one for me even then." She laughed easily. "You can only imagine the daydreams I used to have about him. Thing was, I never saw him again until the day I drove my own food truck onto his construction site nearly twenty years later."

"And Emma wanted cooking lessons," Eva said. "That was how you got in his door, remember?"

Lacy grinned and nodded. "How could I ever forget. Sweet little Emma changed our lives."

They ate more appetizers and had another glass of wine, listening to Darius Rucker—"Only want to be with you"—and tapping their feet, smiling and drinking. "What about you?" Brynne asked Eva.

"Joe and I met on a date. I set him up with another woman, and I had to tag along."

Brynne wrinkled her nose, trying to make sense of Eva's bold lead-in.

"Quit trying to make it sound so intriguing," Lacy teased. "The other woman was eighty years old." Lacy gave Brynne a deadpan stare, which made her blurt a laugh.

"True," Eva said, standing to dramatize her story. "But she had great taste, and her only wish was to have a date with a handsome man before she lost all of her memory. She'd chosen Joe because, as a young politician, he reminded her of Jack Kennedy."

They all chuckled over her wild story.

"Savannah had a great date, and after we dropped her home, Joe and I went at it like rabbits in the back of the stretch limo."

"No!" Brynne couldn't imagine sophisticated and proper Eva doing such a crazy thing.

"That's how we named Estrella. We'd opened the moon roof and got it on under the stars. First date flat on my back."

"She's our slutty sister," Lacy stated proudly.

"Right," Eva retorted dryly.

"You mean, one time and you got pregnant?"

Eva took a long inhale. "One crazy date."

"Talk about a life changer," Brynne said, trying to imagine the stress it would've caused to find out she was pregnant so soon after meeting a man.

Eva smiled wide. "We worked it out."

"I'll say."

Eva stood and headed for the door. "I need the ladies' room. Be back soon."

"See," Lacy said, after the door closed. "Sometimes life works out just the way it was meant to."

Except for her. Brynne wanted to wallow again, but she quaffed more wine instead and straightened the tiara. "How's my hair look?"

"Never better."

She suspected Lacy was feeding her a line of bull.

A few minutes later, Eva returned with another

large tote bag. "Let's play It's a Wonderful Life," she said, producing three shot glasses, one for each of them.

"Of course it's a wonderful life—we've found each other, life is good," Lacy said sounding like Emma's enthusiasm had rubbed off on her.

"No, no, no. I mean like the movie where the angel granted Jimmy Stewart's wish and let him see how life would've been without his ever being born." She took out a bottle of tequila and put it next to the shot glasses. She also tossed each of them a chocolate mint patty in what looked like a condom wrapper.

"Well, that's the gloomiest thing I've ever heard of," Lacy said, snatching the mint popping it open and cramming it in her mouth. "We're supposed to be celebrating not going deep."

"Under normal circumstances, we would be. But Brynnie here is obviously in the dumps—"

Brynne perked up, trying to look surprised, since she'd thought she'd done a great job of hiding it until now.

Eva stared the truth down on her. "—and she needs to see how important Paul is in her life. So, we're playing It's a Wonderful life with a twist. We're reversing the game and playing how our lives would be if we'd never met Paul, Zack or Joe. Get it?"

"Ah, wow, I'm not sure I want to go there," Brynne, for the first time that night, protested.

"Too bad, we're all doing it."

"Not me, I'm breastfeeding. I'll use wine."

"Okay. So, three shots, take one after each thing you realize wouldn't or would have happened if we'd never met our guys." Eva poured and passed each sister a shot glass, Lacy's got only a splash of wine.

"Okay, first shot." Lacy threw hers back and slammed the empty glass on the counter as if really tequila. "I'd still be working weddings on weekends to make ends meet with my food truck."

"I'd be escaping life, pretending that all work and no play was a virtue," Eva added after she downed hers.

Brynne followed suit, which was easy after the examples her sisters had set. "I would have spent my thirtieth birthday with Mom and Rory."

"Explanation, please," Eva instructed.

"Paul asked me out for our first date on my birthday. He didn't know it was, and I didn't tell him. I was just thrilled to have a date with a man the day I turned thirty. Especially one I thought was gorgeous."

"Did he find out?" Lacy leaned in.

"Not until a couple weeks later, then he insisted he take me for a proper birthday date."

"What a great guy he is." Lacy leaned farther still, almost falling off her chair. Eva caught her and helped her adjust back in the cushions.

"Think again. Our first date was to a huge family function."

"I've never heard of such a thing," Lacy said.

"I can't remember who or what it was for, but you'd think the pope had come to town with all the people there. Coming from just me and Mom all my life, I'd never been more intimidated. But Paul felt obligated to stop in after our dinner, and his family welcomed me, and even though I was super nervous, Paul and everyone else made me feel like I belonged." She glanced back and forth at her sisters. "And it felt good."

"Like I said, Paul's a great guy."

"So's his family," Eva added.

"You know this after one dinner at their house?"

"Snap judgment. It's a gift. Okay, round two!" Eva looked expectantly at Brynne. "You go first."

Brynne threw back a shot and said the first thing that popped into her mind. "If I'd never met Paul—" She clearly remembered the night in the ER when he'd come in with food poisoning—if she hadn't been floated there for the night… "—I would've taken the job in Salt Lake City."

"Oh," Lacy said, "we want to hear more about that."

"First, another round." Eva poured. They drank theirs but skipped their stories. "Brynne, keep going."

"Can we change her sash to Bossy Diva?"

Brynne smiled at Lacy's protest, which easily rolled off Eva. "Only if it's hot bossy diva."

After a quick laugh, she continued with her

thoughts about leaving Cedars in the City. She remembered, "I wanted to change my life, and applied for a job there. Even had my plane ticket. But the night before, I got floated to the ER and Paul got rushed in with severe food poisoning."

"What?" Lacy and Eva said in unison.

"If I hadn't met Paul, I would've gone for the final job interview."

"You mean, even while he was puking and stuff, you fell for him?"

"Nuts, right?"

"And if you'd taken the job you'd be living in Salt Lake City" Eva said.

"This is great stuff!" Lacy rubbed her hands together.

"Another round!" Eva poured. "Brynne, since you're onto something, you go."

The tequila had loosened her lips. "If I lived in Salt Lake City, I never would've met you, Lacy, or delivered your baby, because I wouldn't have been living here. No way would I have left my job in Salt Lake City to take over the bookstore. I would've let Rory have it right off."

"Isn't this a great game?" Eva looked proudly at them.

But Brynne was lost to her thoughts. "I did, you know, just today."

"Did what?" Lacy asked.

"Give the bookstore to Rory, because she was

Mom's spouse, and she should've gotten the store in the first place, not me."

"That's wonderful," Lacy said, chin on knuckles, listening to Brynne's every word.

"I'll be going back to work at the hospital anyway."

"Since when?" Eva asked.

"This morning. I had an interview, and they offered me the supervisor position for the maternal and child ward."

"Fabulous!" Eva blurted.

"And it was certainly obvious that everyone around there respected you," Lacy added.

"It was?"

Both sisters nodded vehemently at her.

"So you'll finally go back to your first love. Nursing," Lacy said, also nursing the last drop from her thimble-full.

"Well, not exactly. I'll be in admin."

"Not labor and delivery stuff?"

She shook her head.

"Is that what you want?" Lacy asked.

It seemed to be the question of the day.

"I'm not sure," she said, staring wistfully into the bottom of her empty shot glass. And dammit, Paul was right!

Some of the giddiness wore off after the sisters ordered a pot of coffee and ate desserts. Several of them. Having been dropped at home first by the driver, sharing sorrowful hugs and kisses with her soon-to-leave sisters, and making an alcohol influenced promise to caravan with them tomorrow as far as Las Vegas. Brynne, on a caffeine and sugar high—was restless.

They'd forced her to admit how much she loved Paul, how he'd changed her life for the better. He'd even tactfully questioned her taking a job that would keep her off the wards with new mothers and babies, which made her angry. How dare he know her better than she knew herself!

Then the craziest realization of all occurred. She enjoyed working in the bookstore, too. Not owning and running one, but working in one. She loved opening boxes of new books, loved watching people get excited by their favorite authors' latest releases. She also enjoyed recommending books to people, having them come back later to tell her thanks, because they'd found a new auto-buy series.

Why did life have to be all or nothing? Why couldn't it be a little of both?

She washed her face and put on a dress she knew Paul liked, then called him. "Hey, are you busy?"

"It's after midnight, Brynne, of course I'm not."

"Oops, sorry." Only then did she look at the time—1:30 a.m. "Can we talk?"

"I've wanted to since lunch. What's up?"

"Face-to-face?"

"Uh, yes. Here or there?"

"I've been drinking, so you'd better come here."

"Be there in fifteen" was all he said before hanging up. Only Paul would be willing to do this for Brynne...because.

In the meantime, Brynne paced, trying to put her thoughts in order.

Maybe the black eye had knocked some sense into Paul. Driving the RV back to Utah for his new friends, who he hoped would one day also become extended family, was the best opportunity ever.

Brynne sounded like she had something important on her mind. He'd had time to think, too, and he was ready to take whatever she'd give him. If she wanted to work admin at the hospital, he'd support her. All he wanted was to be a part of her life. He jumped out of bed and into his car, only stopping to brush his teeth and run his fingers through his hair.

It always pays to be organized. His nona's advice had been given early in his life, and more importantly, it had stuck. He used the speakerphone to make a call to Las Vegas as he drove to Brynne's. Nona wasn't the only one who'd given him advice growing up. *Always be prepared. Make reservations early*, ever-practical Mom used to say.

You can always cancel them, Paul repeated in his head.

One last bit of advice from his father rounded out his thoughts.

Never be afraid to take risks.

* * *

Before Brynne knew it, Paul rang the bell at the back entrance, and she rushed down those steps to let him in.

"What happened to your eye?"

"I walked into a guy's elbow."

"Poor baby," she said, her guard down, lightly touching his huge shiner. Then she quickly turned to jog up the steps.

"I'm okay. Are you?"

He'd caught on to her still being leftover tipsy, even though she'd downed another strong cup of coffee while waiting for him. "Uh, yeah. My sisters and I got a little carried away at our goodbye party tonight."

When they reached the top and crossed the entrance, he tugged on her arm. "I know it must be tough."

"It is." Instead of taking his open-arm invitation, she headed to the kitchen for a tall glass of water. Man, she was thirsty.

He followed her in. "You wanted to talk to me?"

She turned and leaned against the counter after taking several long gulps. "I hated the way we left things this afternoon, and I wanted to let you know I've been doing a lot of thinking since." She was glad she hadn't slipped up and said, "a lot of drinking," instead.

"I apologize for pushing my ideas on you,

Brynne." His shoulder and the door frame held him up. "I'm happy for you with the new job offer."

He looked sad and vulnerable with the black eye, his messy hair adding to her desire to rewind time and take that hug offer. But she had things to say.

"That's just it. After Lacy's emergency, remembering those amazing moments when I saw the head crown and helped deliver Johnny, I could never settle for admin. I'm not meant to be a supervisor. I want to be on the ward, helping patients."

He scratched his jaw, giving her the impression he knew and agreed, but he didn't say a word.

But there was more she'd figured out. "And I need to be in the store helping patrons find the books they want."

He narrowed his eyes and canted his head. "Wait, you're confusing me. Which is it?"

"Both! I want to honor my mother by working part-time in her store, which I've given to Rory."

"What? You really have been making decisions."

"About time, right?" She walked past him, directing him to follow, which, of course, he did. They sat on the couch, both turning toward each other but leaving one cushion between them.

"No offense," Paul said, looking earnestly at her, giving her 100 percent of his attention. "But it's apparent you've been drinking. Maybe now is not the best time to—"

"I know I have, but believe it or not, I'm seeing things clearer now. For instance, Rory deserves the bookstore, not me. It's only fair. *I* can work part-time for *her*."

He opened his mouth, but she barreled ahead, not giving him a chance to speak.

"And while I was at the hospital today, I saw several per-diem positions posted, and one was for L&D. I could work as much or as little as I want, but I'd be doing what I love, not playing supervisor, not sitting through meeting after meeting then diving in to making the work schedules." She looked at Paul, with his sad black eye, and hoped he was catching on to what she was telling him. "Do you know how many people are ever happy with their work schedules?"

Of course he didn't—he loved his job. Obviously baffled by her slightly inebriated monologue, Paul simply shrugged and waited.

"Zero. Well, almost zero. And whoever doesn't complain, everyone else figures is the supervisor's favorite. It's a no-win situation every single month the schedule comes out. Trust me. I know from eight years' experience."

Paul leaned forward and put one hand on Brynne's shoulder. "And this is what you really want?"

"I know how I feel, Paul, and I know what I want. Yes." She finally knew it!

"Then that's fantastic. I'm happy for you."

He gazed hopefully at her, and she could practically read his mind. *Does that include me?* She let him send his secret message a little longer, because, like she'd thought the instant she'd seen him at the back door, he looked so darn sweet, shiner and all.

"Thank you. Glad you see it my way."

"I do," he said, earnestly. "But I'm going to let you sleep this off, and we'll talk tomorrow."

"When?"

"On the road. Will you come with me? It'll give you more time with your family, too."

"My family," she said, her mouth bending up at the corner over the novelty, when up until one week ago she'd thought she was an orphan and an only child. The coffee had her mind spinning and had turned her into a motor mouth. "It seems so odd to say, but now I know how you feel about your big family. And it's kind of great to have a bunch of people who think of me as one of them."

His smile stretched wide, and she wondered if it hurt his puffy nose and eye when he winced and tried to hide it, which endeared him more to her and kind of helped her realize he had a point—she *was* still slightly drunk and definitely overcaffeinated.

"So I'll see you tomorrow?" he said as he stood.

She had the whole week off, no plans, and he was offering a quick turnaround trip to California. And they had so much they needed to talk through. Why not?

"I'll be there."

The guy may as well have been told he'd won the

lottery, from the excited look he gave. "Okay, let's make it a fun road trip."

Just after he swung open the door, he circled back toward her. "Let me get this straight, so I can remind you tomorrow in case you've forgotten everything. You're not going to take the job?"

She shook her head.

"And you're going on the road trip with me?"

She nodded.

"Anything else you want to get off your chest?"

"I promised Lacy and Eva I'd go as far as Las Vegas with them, because they're planning to stay there tomorrow night. Then when they go home Sunday, I'll drive back here."

"Well, that's interesting, because I promised Zack I'd drive the RV back here once they make it home to Little River Valley."

"All that way to California?"

"It's not as far as you think. Only five hundred miles. The thing is, I was hoping you'd join me the whole way."

"Go all the way to their houses?"

"Yeah, don't you want to see where and how they live?"

"Well, yes, but…"

"After, we could take a short vacation together. You said it yourself—it's been an extremely stressful week. We could relax and enjoy ourselves, away from all our normal responsibilities. Maybe stop at

Hearst Castle and take an entirely different route back home? Sightsee."

Her chest tightened. "Why do you always do this to me?"

"Do what?"

"Pull stuff out of nowhere."

"Because we miss opportunities if we don't take chances. Why not? If not now, when?"

"Next, you'll be saying, 'let's get married while we happen to be in Las Vegas,' too."

He shrugged. "It's an option."

Paul was being way too low-key, and it freaked her out, until he reached for her and kissed her good-night. After lunch that day, she'd worried she'd never share another with him, and as his lips pressed gently to hers, it felt like a little piece of heaven. Something she never wanted to let go of. He wasn't being the least bit pushy with the kiss, either, just tender, yet something simmered with the promise of so much more. When her eyes closed, her head started spinning, thanks to the leftover tequila buzz. Feeling woozy, mid–luscious kiss, she popped her eyes open and got a close-up view of his shiner. Black. Purple. Puffy.

"Poor baby," she whimpered over his mouth.

"You're making me feel a whole lot better," he whispered back, his hands massaging her lower back. Then he kissed her deeper, stirring up unexpected passion.

With her guard down, a surge of empathy for her

guy with the black eye and everything he'd had to put up with this past week took over. Hell, for the last six months! She went along with the kiss, enjoying every second of connecting with him. Paul was the one she wanted to spend the rest of her life with. They had a long drive to hash out the details.

A moment ago, she'd tested him about suggesting they get married on a whim in Las Vegas. He'd only said it was an option. Not a given. Now, the craziest thought popped into her head as her arms wrapped around his neck and pulled him closer. She parted her lips so she could taste him.

If Paul was willing to compromise with her, especially about children, why not?

Chapter Thirteen

Lacy wore a huge flowered baby sling with Johnny secured inside on the sunny Saturday afternoon. The day the sisters were leaving for home. She handed her overnight bag to Eva, who stood on the lowest step of the RV, handing up the luggage to Joe, like a conveyor belt. Then the empty baby carrier.

"Has he proposed again yet?" Eva asked Lacy in a conspiratorial whisper.

Lacy shrugged. "Haven't had a chance to ask. Brynne's with him every time I think of it."

"Well, that's a good thing."

Lacy began her reply...

"If you're going to have a conversation, woman, please step out of the RV," Joe said tactfully and sprinkled with sweetness. "We want to be on the road in fifteen minutes." He checked his watch.

"Okay," Eva said, "sorry. I'll do one last house check."

"I'll go with you," Lacy said. "Maybe we'll get an opportunity to corner him."

"GPS says we've got around a three-hour drive," Zack called back from the driver's seat, looking like a pilot preparing for takeoff through the windshield.

"Did *el jefe* say something?" Joe teased in the RV entrance, hand to ear.

"Har-har. As long as the traffic's good," Zack continued his thought.

The sisters shared a "those guys" smile.

"Well, good luck with that," Joe said. "It's Saturday, and we and everyone else in the state are heading to Vegas." Joe hopped down the steps toward the women, then grabbed two of the three large suitcases lined up in a row.

"Looks like they're still doing some roadwork around the strip on I-15," Eva said after quickly consulting her cell phone. "Might slow us down."

Zack made an appearance at the RV door. "Good thing we're traveling in style," he said, as though a magnanimous king.

"Ah, I see the RV brings out your true personality," Lacy teased from the grass near the sidewalk.

Emma popped her head around the door from where she'd been hanging out in the kitchen area.

"I'm making Dad his favorite for lunch! Grilled cheese!"

Zack extended his arms and smiled first at his daughter, then at Lacy. "I'm the king of my castle, babe."

Eva and Lacy eye rolled together.

"Okay, you have fun with that," Lacy said, just before spying Paul by himself. "And Emma, you wait until I'm around to supervise for that sandwich, okay?" She didn't wait for an answer. "Come on, let's hit it!" she said to Eva with an excited whisper as she grabbed her by the arm and dragged her toward their mark.

Ever since Paul had rolled out of Brynne's bed that morning, he'd been on the run. He'd felt great all day as he'd gone about his long list of things to accomplish before they left for the road trip. First he went home to pack, and there he made calls, loads of calls. People needed to be on call in case there was a breakthrough with Brynne.

Currently, Brynne was babysitting Noah and Estrella, and he'd just finished putting their bags in the trunk. He glanced over his shoulder at two redheads rushing his way and smiled.

"Did you propose again?" Lacy said, after she was within whispering distance. Had he been acting that obvious?

He tilted his head, wondering how best to explain it. "Well, not in so many words. But I got a nod."

"A nod?" Eva, also tilting her head, repeated.

"Yeah." He leaned against his car with his arms folded. "We had this unspoken-agreement thing."

Lacy shook her head. "That's not good enough."

"Well, it is for us. For now."

"You're positive?" Eva said, staring at him until he wanted to squirm.

"Let's just say, from my end, it's all systems go. Plus, we've got a long trip ahead with plenty of time to talk."

"Just in case, we have the dress," Eva confirmed.

"And the shoes," Lacy said.

He hadn't put them up to anything, but these two seemed hopeful they'd see their sister say *I do*.

"You've got three hours in the car with Brynne," Eva said, one hip jutting out, arms folded. "It might behoove you to actually say the words and get a verbal response. Preferably something along the lines of, *will you* and *yes*."

"Yes, ma'am." Paul saluted, feeling silly, since he'd never done that before, but Eva had drawn it out of him.

Lacy did her little clappy-hand thing. "I can't wait!" She turned to Eva. "Our baby sister might get married tonight."

Seeming satisfied with their info-gathering mission, Lacy and Eva were about to walk off.

"I've got reservations for an early dinner where you booked our hotel rooms. We'll call it a farewell dinner."

"Sorry it's off the strip, not one of the biggies," Eva said. "but last minute and all, I wanted everyone to stay at the same hotel."

"This'll be great!" Lacy clapped her hands.

"What will be great?" Brynne asked, walking up with one hand holding Noah while he toddled along and the other clasping Estrella tight on her hip. Paul thought what a natural she was with kids. His heart swelled with love—until he saw those big blue eyes grilling him for an answer.

"Oh, I was telling Lacy and Eva about the farewell dinner tonight."

"Oh," she said, her face softening after his reply.

Eva retrieved Estrella from Brynne. "Even though it's going to be so sad to say goodbye."

Lacy and Brynne nodded in agreement, then they attempted a group hug, with the kids adding to the circle size and awkwardness.

"Hey, hold that pose a sec. Let me take a picture," Paul said as the three waited patiently for him to find his phone and snap the shot. Once done, he glanced at the picture first and gave a thumbs-up. Three identical women squinting in the sun but grinning happily, wearing different clothes and hairdos to help tell them apart. They were surrounded by three kids. Johnny, a big bulge hidden inside a loud patterned sling, Noah looking toward the *big twuck*, as he called the RV, and Estrella playing peekaboo while perched on Eva's hip.

In his mind, it was the most beautiful picture he'd ever taken.

"Are we ready to go?" Zack called from the RV door.

"How about one last bathroom break for everyone?" Eva called back.

"Roger that," Zack said.

Two hours into the drive, as Paul and Brynne got closer to Las Vegas, traffic came to a standstill. The change woke up Brynne. Thanks to her overdrinking last night, then entertaining Paul for several hours into the early-morning, she'd fallen asleep on the road within the first half hour. Which hadn't given Paul the right time or moment to talk like he'd hoped.

"Are we here?" she asked, sleepy voiced.

"Not yet, honey. I think it's going to be bumper-to-bumper from here on in, though."

She stretched. "Wow, how long was I out?" She glanced at her watch. "The whole time?"

He smiled lovingly at her. "Just about."

"Not much company." She reached over to squeeze his hand resting near the console, while he continued to steer with the other.

"Well, you sure were last night."

That got a coy smile out of her.

The RV was a few cars up, and Joe and Eva were still right behind them. He could practically feel Eva's single-minded thoughts drilling into his brain. *Propose again!*

"Have a good sleep?"

"I feel human again, thanks, yes." She took the water bottle he'd put into the cup holder for her and sipped.

"Can you remember what you told me last night?"

"About what? What'd I say?"

"Nope. That's what you've got to tell me so I'll know you remember."

"Um, something about you being right?"

He nodded. "Now you're on track. What was I right about?"

"The job." She said it like a teenager. "I'd die being a supervisor. So I'm going to apply for one of the per-diem jobs in L&D and sign on for shifts that suit our plans."

"Wow, our plans. I like how you've really given this some thought."

"Plus, I'm going to work part-time at the bookstore, because I enjoy it, but don't want to run the place. That's after I have Joe handle all the legal stuff transferring ownership to Rory."

"And she's on board?"

"Absolutely."

"This is great stuff."

"I know." Brynne pointed to the traffic. "But this isn't." She gave a long sigh. "Still, this'll be fun."

"Visiting Vegas?"

She nodded. "My first time."

"Want to make it unforgettable?"

"What do you mean?"

What the heck, it was no secret how he felt—may as well go for it. "Will you marry me?"

She went quiet, staring at him, her face unreadable. Did she love or hate the suggestion? Was she about to scream at him or throw her arms around his neck in joy? He had no clue, so he held his breath and waited. This re-proposing was the hardest thing he'd had to do, ever. Except for the first time he'd asked her to marry him eighteen months ago. When he finally needed to take another breath, he said, "I happened to bring the ring." He patted his shirt pocket.

"Is that so?" Noncommittal and far too calm to trust.

He nodded, still waiting and wondering. His stomach and chest tightened, and he put both hands on the wheel for a good strong grip to steady himself.

"We've got a lot to talk about first," she said.

"I know."

"You do? Good. So, first off, you don't get to call all the shots."

"We'll be a team. I promise."

"I'm not promising a kid."

"Why not?"

"I'm scared of motherhood, don't know what it'll look like for me."

"No one does."

"What if it's only like my job?"

He reached over and squeezed her arm. "I know you too well, Brynne."

"Are you willing to wait a year or three while I figure it out?"

"If that's what you need." The hardest words he'd ever spoken, but he'd promised to compromise."

She gave a disbelieving gaze.

He tilted his head. "Not my ideal, but I want to work with you."

"If we did have kids, we'd have to work out child-care."

"My mom would be perfect for that job."

"And Rory."

"Yeah, the more backup the better."

"When I'm ready."

"Yes, ma'am."

"And we pick out our future home together."

"Absolutely."

"No matter how long it takes."

"Okay. Oh, and back to childcare. If, and I know it's a big if, we do have a kid, I'd be willing to pull back on my professor goals. If it makes you happy, I'll be happy to work my schedule around our child-care needs. In other words, it wouldn't all be on your back."

She gave a sideways incredulous glance. "You've been doing a lot of thinking."

"That night in the rain, when you mocked me

with your check, check, check talk, well, you got through to me."

"Wow. You've come a long way in a few days."

"So have you."

"Well, we've had six months to get here."

"And speaking of six months, will you marry me?"

The bumper-to-bumper traffic had opened up and he stepped on the gas, aware there was dead silence from Brynne. He glanced her way, but she looked like she was preparing to play poker in Las Vegas. He couldn't tell if he'd blown it again, and his pulse jumped at the thought.

Finally, a smile cracked her stern expression. "We only live once, right?"

"That's the truth."

"Okay. Since we see eye to eye on the crucial things, and I love you, with all your flaws."

"As I do you," he quickly jumped in.

"I say yes."

He honked the horn and yelled, "Woo-hoo!" And one car back, through the rearview mirror, he could see Eva cheering. Then Joe honked his horn, too. And soon everyone around them started honking their horns, but for a completely different reason. They'd come to another complete standstill.

Everything came crashing down on Brynne that evening while sitting at the long restaurant table surrounded by her sisters and their families. Paul's parents, one of his siblings and Nona showed up, Her anxiety reached a new high. Taking her for granted, he'd admitted when they were checking into their room, to having his family on standby all morning. Which made her wonder how much more he'd planned?

Appearing from what seemed like nowhere, his family waved at her, came by to say hi and kiss her cheek where she sat, then joined the crowd, pulling up chairs and disrupting the waitress from taking their orders. Pressure pushed on her temples and heart.

Too much was going on, He'd wasted no time in arranging for their wedding that night. She understood the unusual circumstances, and his wanting to take advantage of having her family together for the event. But now this, his family showing up. Now the pressure spread to her chest. There was also everything that had happened in the past week that had led up to now. Plus, the thought of saying goodbye to her sisters after only just discovering them. Grappling with all the changes made her world and life spin far out of her usual comfort zone. She simply couldn't handle it. As everyone chatted excitedly—Lacy her usual animated self, Eva the observer, assessing everyone—she excused herself for the restroom. Hoping Eva wouldn't catch on to her panic, Brynne headed through the noisy and crowded casino to the nearest exit. Once outside, hit by heat and, at 5:00 p.m. Nevada time, the glaring end-of-day sunlight, her pace quickened until she ran like a salmon upstream, through the pedestrians on the overcrowded sidewalk. Where to? No idea.

What was wrong with her? She wasn't ready to get married. Not tonight anyway. The week had been nuts—she still had much to process. Her sisters were both happily married, she could be, too. But could she have what they had? With Paul?

He'd promised her the moon, would he remember every little detail after they got married?

She kept running across the pavement, toward a small outdoor café on the other side of the street. There were benches to sit on, where a girl could think. Man, did she need to think.

Maybe she was escaping simply because her world, a carefully controlled place she'd created on her own terms, was under siege. A wrecking ball consisting of a fiancé who wouldn't back down, the shock of discovering siblings and their families, and a profession she loved morphing into a middle-management job headed straight at her. Not to mention in-laws, like a gazillion of them on Paul's side alone. Plus the new ones. Everyone seemed to want a piece of her, and soon, if she didn't protect herself, would nothing be left?

It was all too much. He'd only just re-proposed. She couldn't deal with it. Nearly numb with doubt, she stood and got swept into the passing crowd.

* * *

Paul looked up from his cell phone. The confirmation had just come through. The chapel was still theirs at 10:00 p.m., and he'd be there. Along with everyone else. Yes, he replied. He glanced around the table. Brynne's chair was empty. His vision homed in as he examined the group. Finally his gaze came to Eva, who seemed to be waiting for him to notice. She jerked her head toward the door. He pointed in the casino's direction with his thumb to verify. She nodded.

Brynne had taken off not for the bathroom, which would be the most logical destination, but out the front door.

He jumped up. Lacy grabbed his hand to hold him back. Had she noticed, too?

He bent to hear better.

"It's called wedding meltdown. We both went through it. Be understanding." Lacy sounded relaxed, but who wouldn't be holding a sleeping baby? Brynne? Lacy showed him a mug shot of Brynne with a sign: Crime: Cold Feet. He'd never seen anyone look so unhappy in his life.

Eva appeared at his side. "And if she needs backup, we're here for her."

His anxious gut guided him across the room, making him step up the pace until, just outside the casino, he broke into a sprint. Where would she go?

The mug-shot sign had said Bridezilla. Crime: Cold Feet. He'd never think of Brynne, who liked to be in control, as Bridezilla. But the cold-feet part rang true. She'd doubted so much of what he'd wanted for their future. But they'd hammered it out in the car. Finally. He'd stand by those promises. Didn't she believe him?

Running full out, he spied a small café with benches across the busy street. As he passed he asked a couple, "Have you seen a woman with red hair?"

Glancing at him, they hesitated. He'd forgotten about the black eye. Damn! What if they thought she'd given it to him? Or he was a bad guy after her?

"We're supposed to get married soon," he said, trying not to sound desperate.

Apparently, they decided what happens in Vegas stays in Vegas, and who were they to judge a guy with a black eye on his wedding day? Okay, that was a lot for him to assume, but his head was spinning, and he needed to catch up with Brynne. Now! The young couple, having made a decision to help such a desperate guy, nodded and pointed in the direction she'd gone. He followed the flow of pedestrians but did his best to sidestep some and go faster than others, to beat the pace of the crowd.

Finally, up ahead, in front of a coffee shop and boutique, there was another bench. A lone figure sat on it. Brynne. *Thank God!* Racing for his prize, he didn't wait for the crossing light, just shot out into the street, having to dodge a straggling car. Damn. The last thing he wanted to do was get killed on his wedding day. With heart pounding, he continued toward his love.

Brynne was hunched on the bench, head in her hands. Paul clutched at the intense stab under his lower rib cage. It cut deep. He approached her, completely out of breath.

She must have sensed him and looked up, emotional pain covering every inch of her face, while his grimace was thanks mostly to that blasted side stitch from tracking her down, plus a world of worry.

"What's up, babe?" He tried to sound casual, though his pinched tone gave away how out of breath he was, and when did he ever call her babe?

"I don't know. I think I've gone crazy." At least she didn't tell him to stand back.

He dropped to a knee in front of her. "Not you. You're the sanest person I've ever met."

"Then why am I scared to death about getting married?"

His head dropped back at the truth. He squinted against the late-afternoon sun. It was time to be honest, to quit brushing off Brynne's concerns. "Because I'm forcing you to make a decision you're still not ready to make?"

"But I love you." Her tone was weak and completely unconvincing, and his heart joined in with the aching side stitch.

"But apparently you're not ready to get married." He hated admitting it.

"Everyone expects me to."

"That's not a good enough reason to go through with it." Was he honestly campaigning against his best interests? And hers, if she'd just see straight and finally realize what a great team they'd make.

"And I love you. I do."

Well, then, at least there was still that. But he needed proof. "Are you sure?"

She hesitated.

"Then that's not good enough for me, sweetheart." He stared at her; she stared back. Was today actually not going to happen? Sadness zinged through every part of him. It was Brynne's call.

"Things got out of hand." She continued to sound weak and unsure, nothing like her normal self. All he wanted to do was support her.

"Your sisters showed up."

"My mom posthumously came out of the closet."

"I gave you an ultimatum." He added to the list. His discomfort was emphasized by his knee being on some gravel.

"Dick."

Ouch. But, yeah, he'd suspected as much. She was still angry at him. "I know. But I'm a dick who loves you. Who just wants us to be together."

"I assumed we'd elope, but there's so many people here."

"Just some family."

"Nona's even here! That's a lot of family."

"I guess I just wanted to make our elopement

kind of like the wedding we planned. Let others enjoy it along with us."

"And that's another thing—you do everything different than me." Her eyes narrowed, she looked confused.

"I'm a guy." Finally the side stitch let up. "You're foreign territory for me, too."

"I want my mom." Surprising him, she cried, and he did what came naturally where Brynne was concerned. He consoled her the only way he knew how, by sitting next to her on the bench and pulling her to his chest, then holding her as she went snotty with tears on his shoulder. They stayed this way for several seconds.

"I wish she was here, too."

"I'm so angry at her for dying."

"Is that part of this?"

"Yes! She left me to go through my wedding alone, and I'm so mad I could spit. She was always supposed to be there. She'd always been my rock."

"But you've got your sisters to help, now."

"Stop! Could you just stop trying to fix everything? I'm sorry for lashing out, but just listen to me. I'm mad at Mom for dying and missing my big day. I've been so busy being mad, instead of grieving, I got stuck. I read an article about mourning and the importance of not rushing into anything after the loss of a loved one. I grabbed onto that bit of information and have strangled it close ever since."

"I'm not telling you to move on or anything, I'm just mentioning it might be a good time to let go of that."

She gave a quick sigh, and he worried he'd pissed her off again.

"I realize I've been transferring my anger at Mom onto you," she said, surprising him. "Because you're the person I trust most in the world now that she's gone."

"Uh, thanks?"

She laughed lightly. "I know, I'm sorry."

"It's okay, sweetheart. I'll take anything you need me to take, because I love you so much." He gathered her close and hugged her tighter.

"I guess this is my twisted way of telling you I do love you."

Finally, no question in her tone! "You've just made me the happiest guy in the world."

Brynne's resistance broke—he felt it. She collapsed against him. "How can I not want to marry you?" she said between sobs and gulps with her face a smeared mess of mascara.

"I'm not sure what that means, but I'm hoping you're going to?"

Slowly and solemnly, she nodded against his shoulder.

"Because you want to?" he recited syllable by syllable.

She nodded again, this time with less resistance.

Maybe they'd made it over the final hurdle.

"I love you," she whimpered to his chest.

"Good. But seriously, we don't have to get married today if you're not—"

"I'm sure."

"Okay." His hands shot up.

"And besides, everyone's here."

Here they went again. He held her out, at arm's length. "I repeat, that shouldn't be the reason."

"I don't want to live my life without you."

He saw it in her puffy eyes, the willingness. "Then I believe you."

They stared into each other's faces, verifying the truth. He did indeed love her, and she loved him back, and today they'd get married to prove it. Then they'd move in together and begin their life. She'd take whatever job made her happy, and he'd be her support system for the rest of their lives. Kids. No kids. Whatever. The realization made him smile. "Now go wash your face. I'll meet you at the chapel at ten."

"Okay."

He pulled her to a standing position, smiling the whole time she rose. When he had her full attention, he winked with the nonblack eye. "I can't wait to get my socks knocked off by that new dress."

Through her drying tears she laughed, then swatted his arm. And he knew all was right with his world, again. Because Brynne was finally going to marry him.

Chapter Fourteen

At 10:00 p.m. on the dot, everyone had gathered in the tiny white twenty-four-hour walk-in chapel, with the unique drive-through tunnel of love. Brynne wore the dress she'd bought online with her sisters just a few short days ago that highlighted her legs, along with the perfectly matched shoes.

Her heart beat erratically as she stood out of sight of Paul and waited for the cue to walk the short aisle. Rory stood beside her in a dress, something she had never seen her wear before, ready to give her away. Lacy and Eva were right behind her—whether for moral support or stationed to keep her from bolting out the door, she wasn't sure. Though she was positive she wouldn't want to get married without them.

Everything in the tiny white chapel was cheesy and overdone, from the wallpaper and the white-backed stained-glass windows to the red carpet and gold-painted pedestals holding plastic bouquets, to the artificial grass and the pink Cadillac parked outside in the tunnel of love with cherubs painted on the deep blue ceiling. But Brynne loved it. Because she cherished the man standing at the front waiting for her to say *I do*.

Traditional wedding-march music started playing through the chapel speakers, and Eva and Lacy cut around her to walk to their seats. Zack, Joe and the kids sat on the bride's side in the two-seater pews, where her sisters joined them. Paul's parents, his youngest brother, Frankie, who had volunteered to be best man, and Nona sat on the groom's side.

Rory, who'd arrived too late to join everyone for dinner, handed Brynne the all-inclusive bridal bouquet then held out her arm to escort her, and the smile she gave came from her heart. Brynne's did, too, especially when she caught sight of Paul's reaction to her as she did her version of how she thought a bride should walk down the aisle. From the look of awe in his eyes, she knew how much he loved her. There was no doubt she loved him, either. Throughout all the chaos in life, she could depend on Paul. He'd never proved it more than the last week.

He smiled at her, black eye shining, a great story to one day tell their kids. Wait. Kids?

They'd make, from this day forward, a good life together, an imperfect and complicated life that would be both challenging and wonderful, but above all filled with love. And compromise. If her sisters could do families, so could she. Mom had known from the start he was the guy for Brynne, and she'd been his biggest advocate. Tonight, Brynne felt her mother's presence and approval, especially with Rory walking her down the aisle. The thought made her eyes prick and water.

In no time at all, Rory slipped her arm away and took her place in the front pew. Eva stepped to one side of Brynne and Lacy the other—good thing, too, because she was beginning to feel weak-kneed. Paul and Frankie faced them, and the music stopped. The official wearing a fancy pastor-style robe began the ceremony.

Soon, she surprised Paul by having brought a ring. She might have seemed like she didn't know why everyone wanted to stop in Las Vegas on the drive home, but she'd come prepared. Yesterday, after the girls' night out, she'd dug through her drawers and found the ring she'd bought for Paul at the beginning of the year where it was still safely tucked away. He wasn't the only one who knew how to plan ahead. The surprise in his eyes when Eva produced it for Brynne to slide on his finger was priceless.

"I do," he said, practically before the official had asked the question, "Do you take this bride?"

When it was her turn to repeat the vows, she looked into Paul's eyes. Then she promised with all her heart to love him for the rest of her life. When he put the ring they'd picked out ages ago on her finger, she lost it, but smiled all the way through her happy tears. And though their first kiss as man and wife turned out to be a soggy one, it was the best kiss ever.

A year later

Brynne had never dreamed she'd have three birth coaches, but next to Paul stood Lacy and Eva, each taking turns to get her through one long and hard contraction after another. Just her luck—or maybe it was payback—hers had been the longest labor she'd ever participated in.

Something told her this contraction might be the final one, especially since she thought she might blow off the top of her head as she pushed like everyone, including the doctor, told her to. She looked at the three faces helping her. First the man she loved more than she could ever imagine, her husband, who looked a bit wild-eyed and downright scared by this whole ordeal. Then she watched her two sisters whom she loved without regret, as though she'd known them her entire life. They'd both been through labor before and gave her the confidence she needed to make it through.

"You can do this, Brynnie!" Lacy kept saying.

"You've got this, sister," Eva encouraged.

When the contraction let up, in a rare moment of clarity, Brynne remembered the lesson she'd finally figured out that her mother had left behind. Their story, the surrogate and her triplets who got separated at birth, was what it was and couldn't be changed. It was one of the millions of confusing stories told in countless families across the world. The lesson was to make the best out of what they'd been dealt, all three of them. The bonus was that they'd found each other. They were family now. Their babies would be cousins and would always be in touch. They'd celebrate birthdays and holidays together and would always have the special connection of being relatives. Nothing could ever change that now.

During the brief lulls between contractions, conversation picked up.

"How are you guys going to work out childcare?" Eva, the pragmatist, asked.

"Brynne takes off the first six months, and I take the second six months. After that, we'll have my mom and Rory help with babysitting to work around Brynne's shifts at the hospital."

"Great planning," Lacy said.

"We'll see how it works out," Brynne said, as it became obvious another contraction was starting.

"No reason you can't do it all, my love," Paul said, smiling down at her. "Now push!"

Holding Paul's hand on one side, gripping with all her strength, with Lacy and Eva holding on to her other hand, everyone coaxing her to give it all she had as it rolled through, Brynne, exhausted and nearly ready to give up, made the final push.

A whole new kind of love overwhelmed her as they put the baby girl on her chest, and she sobbed. Paul did, too. "She's so beautiful," he said.

Her daughter joined them crying, and it was several moments before things settled down.

Eva's radiant smile lit up her face. Lacy beamed beside her, and they joined in the group cry.

Brynne stole glances at her daughter, instantly in love.

Paul hadn't hesitated for one moment when they'd found out she was having a girl and she'd told him her name choice.

She cuddled her baby and said to her sisters, "Meet Jessica. Jessica Taylor Capriati."

After today, another redhead would be added to the Taylor family tree.

* * * * *

Don't miss the other Taylor Triplet romances:

Cooking Up Romance
(Lacy's Story)

Date of a Lifetime
(Eva's Story)

Available now wherever Harlequin Special Edition books and ebooks are sold.

#2767 THE TEXAN'S BABY BOMBSHELL
The Fortunes of Texas: Rambling Rose • by Allison Leigh
When Laurel Hudson is found—alive but with amnesia—no one is more relieved than Adam Fortune. He will do whatever it takes to reunite mother and son, even if it means a road trip in extremely close quarters. Will the long journey home remind Laurel how much they truly share?

#2768 COMING TO A CROSSROADS
Matchmaking Mamas • by Marie Ferrarella
When the Matchmaking Mamas recommend Dr. Ethan O'Neil as a potential ride-share customer to Liz Bellamy, it's a win-win financial situation. Yet the handsome doctor isn't her usual fare. Kind, witty and emotionally guarded, Ethan thinks love walked out years ago, until his unlikely connection with his beautiful, hardworking chauffeur.

#2769 THEIR NINE-MONTH SURPRISE
Sutter Creek, Montana • by Laurel Greer
Returning from vacation, veterinary tech Lachlan Reid is shocked—the woman he's been dreaming about for months is on his doorstep, pregnant. Lachlan has always wanted to be a dad and works tirelessly to make Marisol see his commitment. But can he convince marriage-shy Marisol to form the family of their dreams?

#2770 HER SAVANNAH SURPRISE
The Savannah Sisters • by Nancy Robards Thompson
Kate Clark's Vegas wedding trip wasn't for *her* wedding. But she still got a husband! Aidan Quindlin broke her heart in high school. And if she's not careful, the tempting single dad could do it again. Annulment is the only way to protect herself. Then she learns she's pregnant...

#2771 THE SECRET BETWEEN THEM
The Culhanes of Cedar River • by Helen Lacey
After months of nursing her father back to health, artist Leah Culhane is finally focusing on her work again. But her longtime crush on Sean O'Sullivan is hard to forget. Sean has come home but is clearly keeping secrets from everyone, even his family. So why does he find himself wanting to bare his soul—and his heart—to Leah?

#2772 THE COWBOY'S CLAIM
Tillbridge Stables • by Nina Crespo
Chloe Daniels is determined to land the role of a lifetime. Even if she's terrified to get on a horse! And the last thing her reluctant teacher, Tristan Tillbridge, wants is to entertain a pampered actress. But the enigmatic cowboy soon discovers that Chloe's as genuine as she is gorgeous. Will this unlikely pair discover that the sparks between them are anything but an act?

*When Laurel Hudson is found—alive but with
amnesia—no one is more relieved than Adam Fortune.
He will do whatever it takes to reunite mother and son,
even if it means a road trip in extremely close quarters.
Will the long journey home remind Laurel how much
they truly share?*

*Read on for a sneak preview of the final book in
The Fortunes of Texas: Rambling Rose continuity,*
The Texan's Baby Bombshell *by Allison Leigh.*

He'd been falling for her from the very beginning. But
that kiss had sealed the deal for him.

Now that glossy oak-barrel hair slid over her shoulder
as Laurel's head turned and she looked his way.

His step faltered.

Her eyes were the same stunning shade of blue they'd
always been. Her perfectly heart-shaped face was pale
and delicate looking even without the pink scar on her
forehead between her eyebrows.

Her eyebrows pulled together as their eyes met.

Remember me.

Remember us.

The words—unwanted and unexpected—pulsed
through him, drowning out the splitting headache and the
aching back and the impatience, the relief and the pain.

Then she blinked those incredible eyes of hers and he realized there was a flush on her cheeks and she was chewing at the corner of her lips. In contrast to her delicate features, her lips were just as full and pouty as they'd always been.

Kissing them had been an adventure in and of itself.

He pushed the pointless memory out of his head and then had to shove his hands in the pockets of his jeans because they were actually shaking.

"Hi." Puny first word to say to the woman who'd made a wreck out of him.

Still seated, she looked up at him. "Hi." She sounded breathless. "It's…it's Adam, right?"

The pain sitting in the pit of his stomach then had nothing to do with anything except her. He yanked his right hand from his pocket and held it out. "Adam Fortune."

She looked uncertain, then slowly settled her hand into his.

Unlike Dr. Granger's firm, brief clasp, Laurel's touch felt chilled and tentative. And it lingered. "I'm Lisa."

God help him. He was not strong enough for this.

Don't miss
The Texan's Baby Bombshell *by Allison Leigh,*
available June 2020 wherever
Harlequin Special Edition books and ebooks are sold.

Harlequin.com

HSEEXP0520

Don't miss the second book in the Wild River series by

Jennifer Snow

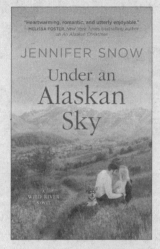

"Never too late to join the growing ranks of Jennifer Snow fans."
—*Fresh Fiction*

Order your copy today!

Be sure to connect with us at:

Harlequin.com/Newsletters
Facebook.com/HarlequinBooks
Twitter.com/HQNBooks

HQNBooks.com

PHJSBPA0520

Love Harlequin romance?

DISCOVER.
Be the first to find out about promotions, news and exclusive content!

Facebook.com/HarlequinBooks

Twitter.com/HarlequinBooks

Instagram.com/HarlequinBooks

Pinterest.com/HarlequinBooks

ReaderService.com

EXPLORE.
Sign up for the Harlequin e-newsletter and download a free book from any series at
TryHarlequin.com

CONNECT.
Join our Harlequin community to share your thoughts and connect with other romance readers!
Facebook.com/groups/HarlequinConnection

HSOCIAL2020